The Dresden Vases

R. J. Ellis

EDWARD GASKELL *publishers*
Devon

Edward Gaskell publishers
Cranford House
6 Grenville Street
Bideford
Devon
EX39 2EA

First Published 1999

isbn: 1-898546-35-5

The Dresden Vases

Printed and bound in the UK by
Lazarus Press
Unit 7 Caddsdown Business Park
Bideford
Devon
EX39 3DX

The Dresden Vases

R. J. Ellis

To Dee with love

The idea for "*The Dresden Vases*" was conceived at a writers' course led by the west country author Roselle Angwin to whom I pay thanks for her helpful suggestions.

I wish to thank Dee for reading an early draft of the story and for her encouragement to continue with the work.

"*The Dresden Vases*" is entirely a work of fiction. The names, characters and incidents portrayed are the work of imagination. Any resemblance to actual persons, living or dead, events or localities is entirely coincidental.

R. J. Ellis
Bideford
Devon
October 1999

Chapter One

Rebecca Radstone was desolate. In so far as she was consciously aware of anything, she believed her life was at an end. Residing at the house of Mrs. Bernadette Lampard in Dublin, she had received early discharge from hospital only because of the safe hands she was known to be going to. She was, in fact, being tenderly cared for.

Rebecca knew she was regarded by Bernadette as a precious daughter whom she loved, but her present state of mind made it impossible to respond to her kindness. Rebecca's traumatic birth-pangs had terminated in a violent experience which had left her physically and mentally bereft. Her emaciated body had revolted at the pregnancy. Her mind had then become overwhelmed with feelings of horror and guilt and she became even more disorientated as her physique gradually improved. She had undergone great emotional upheaval in the previous twelve months and the horror had returned to take further vengeance.

Bernadette brought Rebecca a mug of coffee and they both sat in the summer house on that golden morning in the early Autumn of 1945.

"Tom wishes to come and see me. He will have to stay for a few days. Will that be convenient?" asked Rebecca as she read from a letter just arrived from London.

Bernadette had some reservations but replied with characteristic generosity.

"Of course dear. You feel strong enough for visitors?"

Tom was such an old and faithful friend Rebecca could not imagine him as a 'visitor.'

Within a week of receiving his letter Tom had been admitted to "The Laurels". Though he had been forewarned by Bernadette he had not sufficiently prepared himself for Rebecca's condition. He was flabbergasted when he saw her; the girl he had loved for years reduced to a near-nervous wreck.

Tom brought news from family and friends in London. He remained in Dublin for eight days and thought he saw a small improvement in Rebecca's health. Certainly she was sufficiently self-assured, even if it was mainly bravado, to tell Tom it was high time he went back to see to his developing business. As ever, Tom did what she asked. He returned to Rebecca's parents' house and retailed his account at the seat of exchange, the kitchen table. When Leopold and Rachel first heard his story they were torn with mixed feelings. They were exceedingly glad their only daughter was on the mend; they were grateful to Tom for making the journey. Yet they were still worried about her and would remain so until they had her back in Hampstead Road.

The evening after Tom had left "The Laurels", Bernadette and Rebecca, sitting in the dining room after the evening meal, found themselves staring at each other. For the moment no words were spoken. Then the faintest twinkle of a smile passed between them. Bernadette rose and put her arm around Beccy.

"It will pass," she said.

The women cleared the crockery from the table and moved to the kitchen to wash the dishes.

"And we used to have a maid to do this job," said Bernadette, "Before the war."

"I remember," said Rebecca. "Tom was such an ingenuous boy. Full of high ideals. He even joined the International Brigade in 1937. He was wounded in Spain."

Bernadette found herself in two minds. Glad that Rebecca was taking the initiative in conversation again, but not sure she approved the trend of thought. Suddenly Rebecca crossed the room and enfolded Bernadette in her arms.

"I have been so preoccupied, I've not even given a thought to your worries."

The women clung to each in silence. Bernadette knew Rebecca had to unfold her story in order for the therapeutic process to begin.

Chapter Two

It all seemed so long ago. A social revolution ago. One of Rebecca's earliest memories was of uncomfortable travel with her small brother by road, rail and sea when the family had emigrated from Germany in 1930.

Rachel and Leopold Radstone had found the only accommodation they could afford, a single room in a tenement building off the Commercial Road in the East End of London. They had one relative living in the building, Uncle Ruben, who had arrived in England ten years earlier.

Leopold was a tailor, a trade he had learned from his father. Though his work was drudgery it kept the family just above abject poverty. The Radstones' arrival in England, however, coincided with a slump in trading which had the effect of making their privations more severe. Most people in the district were poor and there was great competition for any employment.

Some of the local residents referred to the Radstones as refugees but Rachel and Leopold proclaimed their naturalisation. They had emigrated legally and were able to fulfil the obligations imposed upon all 'entrants.' They were proud people; they had no illusions and they had not expected the streets of London to be paved with gold. They fully understood that survival would be a struggle, and integration difficult. Leopold cherished the hope that after a period of perhaps five years' hard labour they would have earned a stake in their country of adoption and might be accepted as English; Jewish-English at least.

For Rachel, who had been a housemaid to a Junkers family in Saxony, the rawness of East London was, at first, almost unbearable. She and her husband worked elbow to elbow, at night stitching by candlelight. Coal gas was piped to their room but they could afford to use it only for heating the smoothing irons.

For sleeping arrangements they all had to get together on the floor. Before laying down the blankets Rachel searched the floor for pins by using a large horse-shoe magnet which had once served as the field of a dynamo. On winter nights they huddled together for warmth. In the summer the only ventilation came from the one window which had to be propped open as the sashes were irreparable.

For the children it was not so bad. Rebecca and Joseph generally enjoyed their time at elementary school and for Beccy in particular it was proving to be a successful experience. She was a talented pupil and many of the teachers in this Council School were aware of her potential. Specifically, her gift for languages became apparent. This discovery was made fortuitously in a 'Domestic Science' lesson. The teacher, Mrs. Fisher, who was cultured and dedicated in her regard for her girls, once produced a German menu. To her delight Beccy naturally pronounced the words with a softly flowing tongue. Modern languages did not form part of the school curriculum and Mrs. Fisher was quick to observe the child's fluency.

"Where did you learn German?" she asked.

"My mother speaks it" came the reply.

"Would you like to teach me?" Mrs. Fisher asked of this thirteen-year old girl.

With no sign of embarrassment Beccy said "Yes please Mrs. Fisher."

"If your parents agree shall we stay after school tomorrow? Not more than half an hour."

Rachel and Leopold readily gave their consent and the following day at four o'clock Beccy drew her chair unselfconsciously up to the teacher's table.

"Shall we just try speaking to each other?" said Mrs. Fisher.

"I've scribbled some phrases."

And while the cleaner banged table tops and mopped the chairs and floors with disinfectant, the teacher and the child chatted away.

"Are you crying Beccy?"

"No. It's the carbolic Mrs. Fisher. It's making my eyes run".

"We must stop then. Shall we have another lesson on Friday? We could try the Staff room. Ask your parents."

On Friday they met at the Staff room door. Mrs. Fisher led Beccy in and was alarmed to find it clouded with tobacco smoke. She so rarely used the room she had forgotten how fuggy it was.

"This is choking. Oh no, this won't do. We can't stay in here. Beccy, I live only a mile from the school. If I write to your father giving my address do you think he would let you come home with me? Would you like to?"

"Yes please Mrs. Fisher."

Rachel was delighted a teacher was taking a special interest in Beccy and willingly agreed to the proposition. Leopold wrote to Mrs. Fisher and an arrangement was made. Mrs. Fisher was to return Beccy to her parents after the session. And the sessions gradually became longer; partly because Mrs. Fisher provided tea, but more importantly because the conditions changed. Mrs. Fisher had a very good knowledge of spoken French. The teacher and the child exchanged roles. Beccy learned French, Mrs. Fisher German. It became a most amicable arrangement and continued throughout Beccy's last year of school.

On her fourteenth birthday Rebecca managed to secure a job with a large department store in Tottenham Court Road. Apprenticed to a sempstress she received nine shillings each week. Daily fares accounted for nearly half the money; she gave her mother four shillings and of the remainder she put sixpence each week into her Post Office Savings Book. This account, she was told, would yield two and a half per cent interest. She gave one penny on a Saturday to her brother Joseph and the threepence left she kept in a jam jar. She rarely spent any of the money although there were temptations. In the height of summer when strawberries were in glut the costermongers would try to sell them off late at night for "penny-a-pound".

Rebecca was a diligent girl, bright of eye and quick to learn. She became a studious apprentice and after nine months was given a rise of two shillings. By the year 1936 she was a very socialised Cockney earning eleven shillings a week.

At this time her father made and sold three-piece suits, made-to-measure, of medium quality serge for forty shillings. He bought the cloth in Houndsditch and would return with a roll of material unwrapped, protecting it under his greatcoat if it was raining.

Joseph, two years younger than Rebecca, attended a Trade School. There, he was supposed to learn carpentry and light metal work. Although he was a bright boy and keen to learn he had no feeling for these materials. At home with his father he had progressed to cutting out and stitching trousers and was soon to be allowed on to waistcoats. He was a gentle agreeable boy who was sometimes bullied at school. But he did not complain. In fact he had hopes of becoming a proper Cockney. To the chagrin of his parents he had already acquired the accent.

Joseph had grown tall and thin like his sister. Rebecca really was very slender. At fifteen years of age she looked particularly vulnerable when she squeezed on to the upper deck of the tram car with the early morning workers. She tried always for the lower deck where most of the women sat and where there was no smoking or spitting. But if she had to go upstairs, or 'outside' as it was called, she found it difficult to breath as the atmosphere was blue with the smoke from the rough-shag tobacco. And the heavily-coated men left little space on the wooden slatted seats. Rebecca perched on the edge of the nearest seat, paid her fare when the conductor arrived and was glad when the Kingsway underground tram track had been passed. Then the streets became broader and most of the men left to clump noisily down the stairs. They were soon lost to view heading toward the Strand and the Aldwych.

She too had a fairly long walk when she alighted at Kingsway. Eventually she learned the shortest route to link Gower Street and Tottenham Court Road. With all the walking she sometimes pushed her toe through the foot of her lisle stocking, but at work she could snatch a minute to darn the hole. Her friend once saw her doing this and told her never to wear garters as they were bad for your legs.

"My Mum says they give you varicose veins," she said.

After this Rebecca sewed buttons to the top of her stockings and hitched these to the loops on her liberty bodice. And she still pushed her big toe through.

Sometimes on very cold winter days she walked with her friend to the Whitefield Street soup kitchen, where for tuppence she could buy a large bowl of broth with a hunk of bread. She had three-quarters of an hour for lunch break and whatever the weather the sempstresses were not allowed back into the building until Time. Then the heavy doors were unbolted. The girls and younger women ran up the flights of stone stairs; the older employees trudged up. The work was done on the top floor. The natural light was reasonably good and in the afternoons the gas mantles hissed quietly in accompaniment to the chatter-chatter-chatter of the treadle Singer machines. Rebecca, once promoted to a sewing machine, took to it easily and wished her father could have its use.

Rebecca's employer was paternalistic; the forewoman took an interest in what she called her 'charges.' And if you could stand being patronised, turned in your quota, and never answered back, a very slow but steady progression in the rag-trade was more or less assured.

As Rebecca was painfully thin, Mrs. Elton, the charge-hand, sometimes asked if she was getting enough to eat. She took to bringing her small pieces of cooked meat wrapped in newspaper. Rebecca was not offended, she had not really experienced that mood, but she was embarrassed when she found the small screwed-up newspaper packets poking from her overcoat pocket. The coats hung in a long line of hooks along the corridor. The corridor walls were painted yellow and the broad wooden dado, dark green. One of the young girls running to be on time caught her eye on one of the protruding coat hooks. Thereafter the hooks were raised to be above eye-level and the women had to stand on tip toes to reach their coats. Coat pockets were now well in sight and sometimes newspaper screws could be seen protruding.

There was one lavatory at the end of the corridor. Permission had to be sought to use it. It was an old stone-floored washroom with a bath, a square basin with a cold pipe, and one water closet. On one summer day one of the girls had brought a small bunch of marigolds for the chargehand's birthday. The flowers were put in the sink and later that day were duly presented. The gift was received with thanks and the mild admonition that the sink was not to be used for that purpose as it had to be spotless at all times in case any material needed soaking.

Chapter Three

On Rebecca's sixteenth birthday in July 1936 three wonderful things happened. The Radstones moved. They moved their belongings from their one-room apartment to the ground floor of the same building. Here they had two rooms, a tiny kitchen and their own water closet which they agreed to share with Uncle Ruben.

The second lovely surprise was the news that Joseph was to be transferred to a school of "furniture making" where, in fact, musical instruments were manufactured.

And third! Rebecca was given a bicycle. How they had managed to keep it a secret remained a mystery to her, but there it stood. Her father had painted it shiny-black, oiled the chain and fitted new tyres. The saddle had been covered with an off-cut of carefully stitched serge, and a neighbour, who wove baskets for Billingsgate, had made a small one which was now fitted to the handle bars. Rebecca was overjoyed. Now she would ride her bicycle to work and save the fares. But as her father pointed out, that was to oversimplify economics; where she might save on shoe leather and fares she would have to put by for the replacement of bicycle tyres.

Chapter Four

Rebecca's brother was fourteen when he transferred from the Trade School. By diligent work, good attendance and motivation he had achieved a scholarship to the School of Furniture Making. He hoped to achieve there his ambition to make violins.

Joseph could play the instrument a little. He had never had formal lessons but his father had whetted his appetite. On the rare occasions when the tailoring business allowed, his father would sit on the floor and play a few simple dances. Magyar music usually, some of it quite haunting; and young Joe would wonder at its origins. But Leopold never spoke of this. He had given his son a one-eighth size fiddle for his third birthday. Rachel had made a soft case to protect it but it was usually to be seen hanging on the wall on a nail next to his father's full-size violin. In some ways Leopold had been a good teacher. He never criticised, always encouraged, and as Joe grew older he was able to accompany his father. He never learned formally about 'positions' but seemed to find the right note by intuitively sliding his hand on the neck of the instrument. They never played from written music. Joe did not even know if his father could *read* and he did not himself see formal music until a strange tonic-sol-fah language entered his vocabulary when he was nine years old. When Joe related this to his father it proved to be utterly incomprehensible to him. But his mother caught the idea willingly. She sang along with Joe in a pleasantly soft croon which sent shivers down his spine.

So by seven o'clock on a bright September morning Rachel had Joe cleaned and polished and accompanied him to his place of apprenticeship. He had a knap-sack slung over his shoulder which contained his midday meal. A cup of tea was to be provided. His father had forecast that Joe would be chief tea-boy for quite a while. This turned out to be true and lasted for nine months until the next young apprentice was taken on.

Joe had really wanted to walk to work by himself but had had to compromise. His mother had promised not to step over the works' threshold. She remained at the pavement edge, as agreed, and shyly waved him off. He was framed in the grey-stone portal entrance and she saw that the nape of his neck was hollow. She gave a deep silent sigh. He was painfully thin, like Beccy, but they were both wiry youngsters and had not succumbed to the debilitating influenza epidemic that flourished.

When Joe entered the School of Furniture Making his nostrils were assailed with a cocktail of smells. Glue was warming in a double pot, oil and spirit varnish permeated the air, but over all lay the resinous scent of pine wood.

"Straight from the forest, lad," he was told when Mr. Waring took him on a very brief excursion of the premises. Mr. Waring and a boy not much older than himself were the only occupants, and he learned that the men came in at eight. And when they arrived Joe was overawed. They all seemed to be wearing thick clothes despite the good weather and a new smell was added to the atmosphere. It was as though the very fibres of the timber had penetrated their clothing where honest sweat had first laid claim. And as their boots hit the floor, the boards seemed to give off a mixture of turpentine and coal tar. But these were background impressions. His immediate, all-absorbing task was to fill with water and then balance a huge iron kettle onto a retort stand. Then he lit the bunsen burner. This done he had to match eight tin mugs with their owners. The mugs hung on nails over a wooden drainer and Joe added his own which looked a bit diminutive. He would bring a larger one tomorrow, he determined, even though its enamel was chipped.

Chapter Five

When Rachel left her son at the works' entrance she did not go home directly. One street away from their tenement in Brick Lane there stood a baker's shop; the corner house of a long terrace. Its bare end wall had, perhaps five years previously, presented a resplendent bright cream-coloured facade. But the elements of the smokey East End had taken their toll. Boys had bounced their cricket balls from the wall and lower down, at head level, was a large black patch. Behind this stood the baker's ovens which had helped to discolour the wall. It was onto this patch that generations of school boys had warmed their grubby hands as they passed to and from school. Above the window displayed in green Roman capitals against a gold background was the one word 'Charles.' Charles was the baker. His real name had been Karl Schmidt, and he and his wife had come to England after the world war. They had changed their name to Smith but were known to the present generation as Chas and Maddy.

It was to Chas and Maddy's that Rachel now made her way. She did domestic work for them on two mornings each week, three hours for half a crown, five bob a week. She washed and ironed clothes, cleaned out the bakery and scraped the tins in the outer scullery.

There were perks! According to their lights Chas and Maddy were generous with their tea and buns. But the overriding joy for Rachel was the language; her language. At home with Leo, Beccy and Joe they seldom spoke German. Leo had firmly stated *"Deutsch ist verboten."* Well, not really in such forceable terms! In this mild-mannered family voices were never raised. But Rachel had made the biggest sacrifice because Leo could speak English well, with all the nuances, and the children could pass as native speakers. But Rachel struggled. It was her delight and relief to chatter to Maddy. Maddy still retained gorgeous gutteral sounds which when translated to English caused the children great hilarity. They mimicked her.

"Those Chiltren they crow so I hartly know them."

Rachel enjoyed the morning at the bakery. Hard work came naturally to her and she felt strangely recuperated and ready again to face the daily round with her own family.

When she got home, there would be no surprises. Leo would be at the table cutting out or pressing, or more than probably sitting on the floor stitching. Rachel did some dress-making when she could. As a servant she had learned to darn huckaback towels invisibly, becoming very proficient with a needle.

On the top floor of their tenement building lived a beautiful young woman named Clarence Nagel. Clarence was a housemaid to a family living in Barnsbury. Now, as Rachel quickly learned, London was a strange city, not least for its rapid changes in the character of adjacent areas. Each day Clarence walked up the New North Road to her place of employment. Once she had crossed the City Road the world changed. Fashionable houses with double-fronted windows facing beautifully tended private squares stood proudly announcing their gentility. Clarence had mentioned to her employer that she knew a good dressmaker. And that had been enough. Word had spread and Rachel was never without some 'homework.'

When Rachel arrived home from Chas and Maddy's at midday on that hot September day she kicked her shoes off at the door. This was a family custom. And there was Leo, cross-legged on the floor stitching a lapel. He had recently purchased from a stall near to Petticoat Lane a very ancient Bradbury Family Sewing machine for a florin. Uncle Ruben had repaired it and its polished hand-wheel now looked welcoming as it shone with reflected sunlight. Leo had been delighted with his purchase. A satisfying 'schluck-schluck' came from the long shuttle underground as it made positive accurate stitches.

But today, as Rachel came into the room he was squatting traditionally and hand finishing an edge. Rarely was this luxury demanded and Leo was engrossed in the delicate patterned stitching. Rachel came and stood over him blotting out the light, and slid her fingers into his thick dark hair. He put his work very carefully to one side and very lightly touched her feet. He slid his hands up together, caressed her roughened knees, and loved her.

In the other room there were now three beds. A double bed with brass corner fittings occupied the middle of one wall and against the two others, at opposite ends, were the children's beds.

Rachel and Leo lay across their bed.

Outside a coster was calling "Any rags and bones?" His horse clopped echoingly over the shining cobbles. Leo looked with deep loving at Rachel and she wondered how life could be so good. Leo whispered: "Ich liebe dich."

Chapter Six

When Joe arrived home after his first day as an apprentice he took his boots off at the door, greeted his parents, slumped onto his bed and slept. Leo and Rachel exchanged glances, knowing he would be exhausted and guessing that after an hour he would be asking for supper. In the event, it was twenty-four hours before he regaled them with his activities. At nine o'clock that evening she went to look at him. She undressed him and pulled a cover over him. He did not stir.

Rachel slept only lightly; was awake by five-thirty and prepared breakfast. Usually the meal consisted of bread, beef-dripping and tea. Today she made a saucepan full of porridge oats. She shook Joe awake at six and sat with him while insisting he ate slowly. Although he had missed tea and supper the day before he did not have a correspondingly great appetite. But Rachel made the meal last for twenty minutes. She held a loaf of bread under her arm and cut slices horizontally. She tried to entice him with a sprinkle of sugar on the bread but apart from the porridge he had nothing more than his usual breakfast.

By the time he was ready to leave for his second day at work Beccy was at the door with her bicycle. They were to leave home at about the same time each day. A carrier had been fixed over the back wheel of the bicycle and Beccy asked, half-jokingly, if Joe would like a ride. To her giggling amazement he sat astride the carrier. She fixed the elastics which clipped her skirt hem to her shoes and wobbled off. Leo and Rachel watched them slowly progressing down the street and saw Joe dismount just outside the Citadel.

The parents were not much given to introspection; they had work to do, but they were worried about Joe's exhaustion the previous evening. It transpired that Joe, once introduced to the work bench had been employed all day in the outdoor sheds, turning baulks of timber which were stored for drying and seasoning. Each piece of quartered timber was five or six inches in thickness and had been cross-cut into four-feet lengths. These pieces, he learned, would eventually become the bellies of violins. At the beginning of the day the pieces had seemed reasonably light to turn and stack. By the midday break both his hands were sore and at the close of the day's work he was sick with giddiness and fatigue. He could barely imagine how he had staggered home that evening.

On the following day, with his apprentice friend, Johnny Thompson, they carried on the work from where they had left off. By midday, the task was completed and they reported back to Mr. Waring.

To the huge kettle of boiling water Joe added tea leaves and thus it doubled as a tea pot. After the milk had been allotted the steaming tea was poured into the tin mugs which were then placed on the centre workbench. The men came to collect their mugs and some of them had their own screws of sugar. Mr. Waring had his own cup and saucer and Johnny took it to him in his little glass-windowed office which stood in the middle of the workshop and was reached by a short flight of wooden stairs. From this vantage point Mr Waring could see the whole of the main workshop.

On this day, Joe's second at work, the heat was so great that he and Johnny stayed inside to have their sandwiches. They sat on the floor cushioning their bottoms with rags as the floorboard nails were sticking proud. The three-quarters of an hour break seemed adequate and Joe surprised himself by spending the final twenty minutes outside, sitting among the timber which only yesterday had been his torment. There were hundreds of pieces of wood stored on racks and Joe underwent a new emotion which combined a pride of achievement with the wonder that he was able to do it at all.

At home that evening he was voluble and to his family's great relief regaled them with every conceivable detail of his two days' work. The Radstone family were well used to talking; dialectics seemed to come to them naturally. Around the supper table it was quite customary to argue without heat, to discuss with some regard for objectivity and always to try to reach amicable conclusions. This was a considerable feat considering all four of them were now engaged on a formidable routine of daily work bordering on drudgery.

Chapter Seven

On Saturdays Joe finished work at half past twelve. One muggy day in late November he had arranged to meet his mother. When he stepped outside the building he was immersed in a London 'pea-soup' fog. He found Rachel at the railings, joined arms with her and they proceeded cautiously towards the street market. They found their way partly by memory, partly by blind navigation. Voices were muffled and road traffic largely halted. Eyes smarted and noses ran. One tramcar's bell could be heard clanging hauntingly and one omnibus was being led by a man holding a burning newspaper.

As Rachel and Joe came toward the market, the traders' stalls (with tongues of fire bellowing naphtha flame from their canopied structures) became haloed in ghostly aura. The costers' barrows were shiny with moisture which was exacerbated by the exchange of slippery copper coins. The strongly camphorous-naphthalene vapour, unable to escape the all-pervading fog, stank with throat-clutching oiliness.

Rachel bought some apples at the first stall. Usually she would have made a careful choice by passing up and down the street, feeling, smelling the fruit and comparing prices. Today it was difficult to see anything. But ingrained frugality forced her not to buy any more at the first barrow. Joe held the basket as they edged toward the adjoining stall. The man was calling in the customary way and inviting people to select any bunch of bananas for sixpence. Rachel wanted to make two more purchases; for green vegetables and a chicken. Maddy had said she would put it in the baking oven when the bread came out.

Arm in arm again the two of them slipped and slithered across the wet pavement, bumped into people and were struck across the knees with shopping baskets as they followed the line of flares toward the end of the street. To make their way home they had to cross five or six roads and it was a matter of faith and concentrated listening and feeling that they at last entered their own street. There were thirty six houses to negotiate and Joe counted the gates with one hand while the other shared the weight of the shopping basket.

Rebecca finished work at noon on Saturdays. On this foggy day she did not arrive home until four o'clock having walked with her bicycle. Later that evening the sky began to clear and the ground fog thinned out. Saturday evenings were very special, exciting times for Beccy.

Chapter Eight

Beccy and Joe made their way down toward the docks. Members of the Young Socialists had cleared a derelict warehouse for meetings. One corner of a ground floor had been cleaned and decorated and odd bits of furniture had been installed. A table- tennis top had been raised onto trestles as had a quarter-size billiard table. There was also a darts board. Another set of trestles was in the process of being knocked together in readiness for the expected second table-tennis top. But a special corner of the room was reserved for a circle of motley chairs. This is where they all sat and talked. This was the intellectual heart of the Club. Meetings always took place on a Sunday, but tonight was special; Saturday Party Night.

Rebecca had been a member of the Socialist Sunday Club for a year. She loved attending, contributed wholeheartedly and had many friends. Joining her on party nights, Joe was considering becoming a paid up member; penny for your card and penny a week subscription.

Tonight was to be very special. A wreck of a piano had been donated. It was fairly well in tune and only two keys at the bass were missing. Frank Consett was to play. He was not a member of the Club but he was a good friend and the best musician available. He played without music and everyone's favourite tune was Hogay Carmichael's 'Stardust.' This he interspersed with other tunes. Marian Turner had a side-drum and was getting quite a feel for the rhythm with a set of brushes. After a couple of dances the M.C. Eric Fisher called for 'Fanning The Kipper' in relay teams. Then they had a paper and pencil quiz, a couple more dances, refreshment, lemonade tea and cakes, more dancing and so on.

Everyone at the party was in good spirits when, at about ten o'clock, half a dozen louts wearing black shirts burst into the room, threw the food about, upset the trestles, poured the drinks onto the floor and scorched around pulling the chairs over while shouting and screaming. Then they departed as quickly as they had come.

The shock of the intrusion brought the party abruptly to an end. Marian inspected her drum and tenderly stroked her fingers over the skin. Frank closed the lid of the piano and stood in bewilderment. After a moment or two of eerie quietness, a bucket, a mop and some cloths were produced and they all set about clearing up the mess. Within about ten minutes the place had been restored to some kind of order. There were about thirty people at the party and now they gathered around wondering what to do next. And nothing could be resolved. They locked up the premises, and as they departed agreed to continue the discussion at ten the next morning.

The Sunday Club always started at ten and normally finished at twelve. But sometimes Eric and Dot Fisher, who were in charge, brought some food, usually bread and sausages. All who wished stayed on until about half past one.

The Fishers' only son was Thomas. He was about the same age as Beccy; a most affable boy with a loving disposition. With a ready smile, he would help with anything and he usually did the 'fry up' on Sundays. The group usually numbered about twelve youngsters, aged from eleven to eighteen, with four or five adults in attendance. On this occasion, news had travelled and their numbers were slightly more.

To the usual mixture of banter, seriousness, games, songs and instruction, there was added this morning a sharp awareness of political immediacy. They had learned something of current politics and of the impending trouble on the continent, especially in Spain. They were only too well aware of fascist propaganda through the local activities of the National Front, yet last night's slight fracas had brought generalisation into sharp-focussed immediacy.

On this particular crisp Sunday morning, Rebecca and Joseph made sure they were in good time for their Club. As they made their way toward the docks a Salvation Army Band marched along their street. They followed the band until it halted at the crossroads. A small crowd gathered. The band struck up and the singers proclaimed they were 'Happy as can be, my cup's full and running over.' To add to the merriment as happiness was obviously the theme of the morning's worship, the onlookers recognised among the singers the unmistakable voice and demeanour of one Albert Cooper; the old reprobate who was more commonly seen being ushered out of the *Marquis of Granby*. At the end of the final chorus one man from the crowd asked to general amusement,

"Are you really happy Albert?"

And from the midst of the hollow square he returned,

"Happy? I'm so happy I could ....." and here he paused and searched around the crowd with his eyes, seeking to resolve on an unquestionable superlative. "I'm so happy I could put my foot through that bloody drum."

The crowd roared with laughter as Beccy and Joe hurried off toward the wharf to the dying strains of *'Onward Christian Soldiers.'*

The Sunday meeting room had been titivated and Eric, Dot and Thomas and a few of the regulars were setting out the chairs. The talk centred on the scuffle of the previous evening, and Eric said they would have to try and keep it all in proportion. He reminded them, although they needed no reminding, that most of the walls of the surrounding streets were defaced with graffiti. The I.R.A. signs had been displayed for as long as he could remember. And interspersed with these, more recently, had been calls to support the British Union of Fascists, signed with a lightning stroke surrounded by a circle. And then the Swastika, variously orientated, vied for wall space with 'Buy British' fly-posting. The scene was bewildering, disturbing and ominous.

The Socialist Sunday Club boasted no motto, but inherently stood for the brotherhood of man. Perhaps this was a grandiose concept, especially as Eric and Dot had started the group without seeking, or even knowing, whether they should be affiliated to a larger association. For the time being, at least, they were fairly satisfied with their non-denominational and inclusive rule of membership. Although they could hardly have been called rules. The Club had no written constitution (Eric was seeking guidance on this point) and more often than not, no fixed agenda.

Eric was a fitter by trade and had been chosen as spokesman to represent the shop-floor engineers at Union meetings. He had accepted his responsibility at work almost by default; no one else wanted his job. He was a reader. At any spare moment of the day he could be seen with his nose in a book.

"You can always pick up a book and read," he often said. He had gained the reputation for honest dealing, and was respected by both the management and his work mates. And he was still mildly surprised at the number of people he had found to be sufficiently interested and willing to join him on a Sunday morning. They were people who endeavoured to clarify their own thoughts by discussion and debate.

Dot Fisher who had taught Beccy at the local Senior School shared Eric's taste in literature and had a great love of the theatre. Earlier this year she had inaugurated visits to Regent's Park Open Air Theatre and had secured cheap season tickets for her fourteen year-old girls. They had seen 'The Tempest' and 'A Midsummer Night's Dream' and were clamouring for more. Rachel had been invited to join the drama group and was looking forward to the new season which was to open with a play called 'Tobias And The Angel.' Dot brought a certain lightness to Sunday mornings and was usually able to leaven serious debate with conviviality.

It was to this embryonic group that Beccy and Joe came this Sunday morning. Beccy could claim to be, if not a founding member, then one of Eric's first recruits. And he was pleased that Joe had decided to join them. There was no enrolment ceremony.

Chapter Nine

One evening in December 1936 Robert Moser called to see Leopold, who was characteristically sitting on the floor sewing a coat sleeve of dark blue serge. Moser was a successful young tailor and determined business man. Wishing to expand his affairs he was seeking the services of a master craftsman. Through their mutual friendship with Clarence Nagel he had known Leopold for some two years. He knew him to be an honest, reliable man with many satisfied customers who had recommended their friends to his tailoring.

Leo continued working by the gas light as they talked. Rachel, Rebecca and Joseph were silent and very willing listeners.

"I have taken a lease on a house in Hampstead Road and am putting in five or six men to work on a special clothing order," began Robert.

Leo did not raise his eyes from the material.

"I wondered if you would be the supervisor?"

Leo knew his own worth as a craftsman, but the proposition put before him caused a furrow in his brow. He had never had the experience of delegating responsibility, and he did not know that business was done in this ad hoc fashion. He was wary but gave no outward sign of his thoughts. He glanced up momentarily at Rachel.

"I can pay four pounds a week."

Still Leo did not look away from his work. On the contrary he seemed to be even more absorbed with the stitching.

"Rent-free accommodation of course. It's a bit run down but there is a large work room, a kitchen, two smaller rooms and a recess which has been modified as a bathroom."

Leo did not reply, and Robert looked at the others for some sign of encouragement. But they all remained silent.

When Robert Moser left them there was an outburst of talk.

"Whereabouts in Hampstead Road, Daddy?" asked Beccy who felt she knew the area well.

Leo had serious doubts about coping with the responsibility. The others pretended seriously to consider all aspects of the proposition.

Joe left to find Uncle Ruben and brought him down to join in the discussion.

Rachel and Beccy were fairly bubbling with excitement, saw no impediment, but everything to gain. The men were more conservative. They tried logically to balance the advantages with the disadvantages.

"A bathroom!" said Beccy.

"I do not know the workers I should have to supervise. If their work isn't up to scratch what will I be able to do about it? What if I can't keep up with the orders?" Leo had a fear of producing shoddy work.

Uncle Ruben said,

"It will be better than living here," as he scanned the room.

On the following evening Leo called on Robert Moser and agreed to accept his invitation to inspect his premises.

"But I am not at all sure of the outcome," said Leo, "Rachel will have to have a good look."

Robert was already paying rent on the property so he was very anxious to make a start. "I will take you there on Sunday afternoon," he said.

Chapter Ten

O n Sunday Robert called for them with his Morris Ten. The Radstone's were all agog at the prospects. The premises were found to be situated at the western end of Hampstead Road. Here, the large houses had been separated into flats. This particular house had four storeys; a gate led off the pavement into a small concreted area which gave access to a flight of steps descending to a semi-basement. A grander flight of steps led up to an imposing fan-lighted door. The Radstone's strained to peep through its glass panels as Robert struggled with the keys.

Inside, a dark hallway exposed a floor of peeling brown oil-cloth. Two room doors on either side led off from the hall, with a frosted glass panelled door at its end. The first door on the left opened onto a double room which had a large window aspect on to the main road. Painted in coloured lettering at the top of the window, but appearing reversed in the room, was the legend: "AS YE RIP SO SHALL WE SEW." As they had arrived at the premises by car, which had been left around the corner in Euston Road, they presumed correctly that the sign could be read comfortably only from the upper deck of a passing bus. Obviously this had been used as the workroom. Evidence of tailoring littered the floor: needles and pins, pieces of cloth, knots of thread and cotton reels. Propped against one wall was the wreck of an adjustable tailor's dummy.

They inspected the kitchen with its fitted wooden dresser. There was an open stove, sadly deprived of black lead, and a deep sink with two taps and a wooden draining board.

"There is room for a large table," observed Rachel.

They were intrigued with the brass electric switch mounted on the wall and were only slightly disappointed that manipulation of the switch summoned no light. Robert explained that even had there been a bulb in the socket it would not have worked because the electricity supply had been cut off.

At the end of the corridor was the bathroom. The chipped, enamel bath, centrally placed, was supported by clawed cast iron feet. To either side was a wash hand basin and a water closet. The other two rooms were quite empty and presented bare floor boarding and peeling wallpaper.

Their inspection completed, they were unusually silent as they squeezed into the car for the return journey to the East End.

Chapter Eleven

On the following Saturday Thomas Fisher celebrated his nineteenth birthday. He borrowed a fifteen-hundredweight Bedford van from a friend, and in only two journeys transported the Radstones total effects to the premises in Hampstead Road.

By midday they were all busy with brushes and cloths cleaning the walls, floors and windows. In one corner of the workroom a space was prepared for Joe's mattress as it was agreed that Beccy should have the larger of the two bedrooms until such time as it could be divided.

As the winter afternoon drew on candles were lit as the electricity had not yet been restored. There was a gas fire in the workroom which, on feeding the slot machine with pennies, gave off a cheery glow.

Tom stayed until late. "Now I'll be off," he said finally. "Only four miles to go."

"Four worlds," thought Leo, "of Trade, West End grandeur, of commerce and then the Jewish East End."

Tom shook hands with everybody, a custom he had learned from the Radstones.

"Kiss," said Rachel, giving him a big hug. "You kiss him," she said to Beccy.

Beccy grinned and kissed him. "Not much fun for a birthday," she said.

"Best I've ever had," he said as he ran down the steps.

When she returned to the candlelit kitchen they all held hands, standing by the wooden table and wondered what the future held.

On the following day Beccy cycled back to attend the Sunday Club. Joe stayed with his father to help sort out the cloth which Robert had brought. Leo drew up a provisional worksheet and Rachel continued to scrub and clean in between getting some food onto the table.

The kitchen range needed coal. Rachel found a very small supply in a bunker in the back yard. She scraped it out with a shovel and carried it to the kitchen in a bucket. The stove seemed smokey and unwilling at first but was coaxed to life and the tall chimney gradually pulled a roaring fire. The novelty of having a little hot water at the sink gave a great deal of pleasure.

Robert was as good as his word. Electricity was restored the next day and he arranged for two hundredweights of 'best nuts' to be delivered for firing. He introduced three men and a boy who were to work under Leo's direction and by elevenses on Monday they were all busily engaged. The assistants left at six that evening. After supper Leo returned to the workroom, took stock, tidied up, prepared the next day's work and then, as if by force of habit, sat on the floor and continued sewing. It was not until Joe came to make up his bed that Leo went to join Rachel.

Chapter Twelve

Beccy's workplace in January 1936 was a scene of frantic preparation of gowns and costumes for their Easter Show. At the last moment, before the fashion parade, the organisers found themselves unable to maintain the sequence without the services of one more mannequin. Too late to hire a professional from outside, they wondered whether anyone in the sewing room could be pressed into service. The manager had noticed the slender figure and good deportment of Rebecca Radstone. They were so desperate to model a special item. Would she fill in?

They dressed her in a pyjama suit made from black silk and pinned a huge cartwheel of a bonnet on to her thick raven hair. The hat was made of straw, trimmed with pink roses interspersed with flowing white chiffon; an impossible creation invented to cause gasps at Ascot.

There was very little time for rehearsal. Beccy's turn on the catwalk was brief. It was her sole appearance but the event was to change the whole course of her life.

Shortly after returning to the workroom, where she was greeted with a bombardment of excited questions, she was summoned by one of the buyers who escorted her back to the showroom. Here she was introduced to Mrs. Bernadette Lampard who had taken an immediate liking to the 'black cat with a hat.' Beccy realised immediately she was talking to a person of culture, and with a maturity beyond her years was able to discuss the finer points of haute couture, witnessed, as it were, from the seamy side. Mrs. Lampard listened courteously but responded quickly, with a non sequitur that caused the girl to catch her breath.

"Would you consider becoming my travelling companion?" she asked directly.

Recovering instantly, Beccy mentally interpreted this to be a euphemism for parlour maid and demurred. "Well, think carefully about my proposition, and if you are interested call to see me tomorrow at seven." She gave Beccy her address in St. John's Wood, smiled, and left.

Chapter Thirteen

When Beccy returned home from work that evening she was not at all surprised that Thomas Fisher was there. He had engaged himself as architect, builder and decorator for the Hampstead Road premises. He had formal qualifications for none of these activities but he was a good handyman, loved the Radstone family, adored Beccy and was resolved to help them as much as he could in his spare time.

Her latest news gave them all much to think about and discuss over supper. Tonight the table was illuminated by candles. The electricity was working but they enjoyed the intimacy and slightly mystical quality of candle-light. There was no religious connotation though. Leo had many years ago given up the struggle on the impossible demands made by Judaism and was content to remain agnostic. Rachel would have gone further, to complete atheism, but she saw *that* as having, by implication, the seeds of a religion. So largely she went along with her husband's agnosticism, and the trappings of organised religion hardly affected their lives. And yet!, and yet!, they all loved the candle glow. The light gave off an aura of affectionate family involvement and invariably accompanied a kitchen meal when special considerations were to be weighed.

It was decided that Beccy should keep her appointment with Mrs. Lampard for the following evening. They had all pondered the proposition; a 'travelling companion,' really, it could mean almost anything. There were a hundred questions that needed answers; some of them were given an airing, several times. But no conclusions could be drawn. In the last analysis Leo and Rachel knew they could rely on Beccy's good judgement. One decision, at least, was established; that Tom should escort her to St. John's Wood.

And when 'tomorrow' finally came it rained all day. It did not ease off in the evening; on the contrary, the wind increased and Beccy and Tom were soaked by the time they had walked around the outer circle of Regent's Park. When they found Mrs. Lampard's apartment Beccy implored Tom to go straight home, but he insisted he would wait for her outside.

Beccy was met at the door by a maid who took her dripping coat and soggy hat. She was ushered into a small drawing room, furnished very tastefully, she thought, and Mrs. Lampard standing to greet her. She was invited to take off her shoes and jacket which, despite the best efforts of her gaberdine raincoat, were wet. The maid was summoned and these articles were removed for a semblance of drying.

Mrs. Lampard came straight to the point. She was a professional art dealer, specialising in oil paintings, although she took on all kinds of commissions including the purchase of water-colours and, though rather more rarely, porcelain.

"I am a very busy person; I spend more time away from home than in it. I need someone I can trust implicitly to accompany me."

Beccy tried to pick up on all the unspoken signals and remained silent.

Mrs. Lampard continued. "My need is immediate. And I have to be in Edinburgh in a week's time."

In discussion it transpired that her real home was in Dublin, to where she went as often as her business engagements would allow. The question of wages was broached, together with some personal details. Although Mrs. Lampard had not sought a character-reference she gained sufficient evidence from Beccy's employer to confirm her own opinion of the girl.

"The position is yours if you wish. You would have to take up residence here with me in two days' time. Shall we try a month together? See if it works out?"

Beccy agreed immediately. The family had advised her as to the kind of remuneration and conditions to be sought. And on the face of it Mrs. Lampard's offer exceeded all expectations. Her proposed wage of five guineas a week would be greater than the total earnings of the Radstones, and in addition she was to have accommodation and meals provided.

More than an hour had passed when Mrs. Lampard said "You had better find your clothes now. Speak to Joan. She will tell you all my faults."

Dressed in rather drier clothes now, she had dismissed an offer of a taxi ride home. The rain had slackened and she was bubbling to tell Tom about the interview and her decision. But as she took his arm the feel of his soaking coat and the sound of his squelching boots took away some of her exuberance. Tom was obviously not elated about Beccy's decision; she put his lack of warmth down to his present discomfiture. Despite their fairly fast walking, they took nearly an hour to get back to Hampstead Road. And then Tom declined the invitation to come in.

"See you tomorrow night," he said, as he trudged off toward his home.

The following day Beccy gave notice to quit her employment. To her surprise a couple of her workroom companions shed a tear and then she cried too. She received her wages, minus a day's pay, and returned home in the early afternoon. It was an eerie sensation, milling with the London crowds, and she wondered why so many people seemed to be on holiday. She had thought the afternoon-streets should be quiet while industry proceeded behind the high walls of the factories. She felt quite forlorn and did not recover her spirits until supper time. Then she gradually regained her confidence as her provisional plans were envisaged and discussed by the assembled family.

Chapter Fourteen

I t transpired that Mrs. Lampard had been widowed in 1919. She had one son, George, whom her husband had never seen. She had struggled in these early years to make ends meet. Her father had been an art dealer and she had been involved, on and off, with the business since early childhood. She had learned a great deal vicariously and had later studied at the Slade. After the war there had been a steady upturn in the trading and movement of valuables, particularly with artefacts not connected with jewellery. She had found her forte in transactions concerning the importing of oil paintings and had, by dint of honest and reliable dealings, gained a reputation in the world of art as a reliable authority.

Mrs. Lampard's enemy was time itself. She needed a personal assistant to relieve her of the myriad things she found to be disruptive. She made her hobby her work and thus she was never on duty and yet never off. And now, her well trained eye had discovered Rebecca Radstone; certainly not an empty canvas, and she felt a positive sense of well-being with the connection. Time would tell, but she had always been a good judge of a picture.

She was not to be disappointed. Beccy joined the enterprise wholeheartedly; enjoyed the hustle and bustle of travel, never complained of the hours which were devoted to any project and was a very willing and able student under Mrs. Lampard's tutelage. As part of the contract Mrs. Lampard had promised that Beccy should have at least twenty-four hours off after returning from travelling. Beccy was thus able to regale the whole family with the excitements, anticipations, disappointments and achievements attached to buying and selling works of art. These days the family inevitably included Tom. He was constantly at Hampstead Road discussing his plans for renovating the property. Leo was too absorbed with the day-to-day running of the business to spend much time thinking about alterations and Joe was too wrapped up in his own work. But Tom had a very willing audience in Rachel and Robert Moser. Robert was the owner, after all, and he was keen to develop the business with expanded premises.

When Beccy had been with Mrs. Lampard for some seven or eight months she saw her frowning over her accounts book.

"You are screwing your eyes. May I see?"

Mrs. Lampard moved her shoulder for Beccy to look over. The ledger work would have caused nightmarish alarm to Beccy's father and she had similar feelings.

"Might I be allowed to tidy up the book keeping?"

Mrs. Lampard was at once relieved and delighted. She was now familiar enough with Beccy's abilities to entrust her implicitly with the preparation for the yearly auditing. And Beccy had, with certainty, made her services indispensable.

Later that year the auditor was most agreeably surprised with the presentation, congratulated Mrs. Lampard on her accounts and forecast a steady increase in her investment. Mrs. Lampard asked Beccy to give herself a raise in terms of monthly salary and thought she was being insufficiently demanding when a figure of thirty guineas was settled.

Chapter Fifteen

Several visits were made to Edinburgh that year, and one to Dublin where Beccy was introduced to Bernadette Lampard's son. He was tall, clean-shaven, with a mop of red hair; about nineteen. Beccy was the same age but thought he behaved as though he were much younger. He had been cosseted by doting grandparents who had looked after him during his mother's many absences. He had been sent to boarding school, was now at Trinity and from all accounts idling his time away amicably.

"So you're the one looking after the mater," he drawled.

Beccy had never heard the word 'mater' affixed by an article before and smiled broadly. She was glad though, to have her business credential confirmed.

The ladies returned almost immediately to St. John's Wood and spent several hours in detailed preparation for the following week's activities. Then they separated; Bernadette for two nights with friends in Surrey, and Beccy to the bosom of her family. She had such travellers' tales to relate. After a great deal of cross questioning and giving answers that never seemed fully satisfying they all quietened down and, as was their custom, held hands around a candle-lit supper table.

Beccy was delighted to see that Tom had completed dividing the large bedroom and had decorated the whole interior of the premises.

Joe had been able to vacate the workshop floor in favour of a room of his own. The overflowing workshop had now expanded into its four corners, to everyone's relief. The workmen had been very willing to cooperate with Robert Moser's plans and to learn from Leo. He had risen to the challenge and surprised himself with his powers to organise and delegate responsibility while still cutting to the standard of a master craftsman.

Rachel was not quite so jubilant. She much approved and appreciated living in Hampstead Road, but as the tailoring business expanded, she found her services for stitching and pressing to be more in demand. She no longer left the premises to work outside, and only rarely, went back to Commercial Road to see Chas and Maddy. On her last visit they told her of the hooliganism visited upon them and of the mindless damage caused to property. The glaziers were making a thriving business from the Black-Shirts' activities.

At supper that night Beccy kept her most important piece of information until last. And now it was out! Her next journey with Bernadette was to take her to Berlin.

Rachel stopped in mid-serving and Leo was visibly moved. "Berlin?" he whispered hoarsely, and stood up from the table. Everyone was alarmed at this undemonstrative man's sudden gesture. He could not believe he was hearing correctly and asked again: "Berlin?" Upon confirmation he slithered back to his chair looking horrified. Beccy left the table and stood by her father with her arm around him and her head touching his. Nothing was said for a few moments; then Leo's muffled "No, please. Not Berlin."

The following morning Leo rose very early and was in the kitchen when Beccy appeared for breakfast. He wanted to apologise for his behaviour of last evening and to say that, of course, she must do what ever she thought best. After all, she had made good progress in her cooperation with Mrs. Lampard and he had every confidence in her ability to look after herself.

"Please take special care," he said. "It's not quite the same over there". And he elaborated on the potentially explosive political position in Germany, which had come as no surprise to him. He and her mother had foreseen some of the problems, seized their opportunity years ago and through times of great privations had made a new world in which to bring up their two children.

Beccy had no words. Although she knew something of their background her parents rarely spoke of it. But still she had not anticipated the strength of her father's reaction to her projected journey.

Leo was in the workroom when Beccy came to say goodbye.

"I'll be like the bad penny. Love you Daddy."

Everyone wished her well and begged for all the latest news when she returned. Rachel walked with her until they reached their favourite seat near the Botanical Gardens. It was a glorious morning in the early spring of 1937.

Chapter Sixteen

The two women left Croydon and flew by Imperial Airways to Paris. Beccy was so thrilled with her first air journey that the thought of the hotel accommodation she had arranged went quite out of her mind. She had booked to stay three nights at an hotel near the Gare du Nord, but upon arrival she had some misgivings about her choice.

The hotel looked distinctly shabby and she caught Bernadette's look of mild disapproval. But they installed themselves quickly and separated. Bernadette had some business to attend to and left Beccy to her own devices. She went directly to the Latin Quarter. She walked about for hours. She was a natural linguist and was delighted to be able to practise speaking colloquially. The language seemed to trip off her tongue and she found her first visit to Paris a hugely enjoyable experience.

That evening Bernadette stated she was not satisfied with the hotel's service. She appreciated Beccy's house-keeping but thought they could be a little more expansive when abroad. Consequently, the following day they paid their bill and removed themselves by taxi to a hotel in Rue St. Honore. They quickly disposed of their luggage and rehearsed the day's arrangement. They would visit the Louvre, where Bernadette was to meet a prospective client, or his representative. Then they were to view a picture at a private collection in the evening.

In the event the meetings were not overtly successful, no sale was achieved. But it had been a very interesting experience for Beccy. She was amazed at the number of people who greeted Bernadette as a friend, and by how she was received everywhere as an established connoisseur. Beccy was carefully observant, rarely spoke unless first addressed, deferred graciously to her employer's wishes and learned rapidly. She was able to retain accurate information, writing it in note form when back at the hotel, and was able, to Bernadette's delight, to give accurate comment about the material they had seen. And this information was carefully developed to depict market trends. Together, the women were channelling a profound knowledge of the art world into a profitable venture.

They enjoyed one more day in Paris before flying by Junkers three-engined aircraft directly to Berlin. A taxi took them to the Glockner hotel where they were given adjacent rooms overlooking the Konstanzer Strasse.

Chapter Seventeen

The Glockner had an air of Edwardian grandeur. Oak panelling lined the walls on which were discreetly draped heavy tapestries. Bernadette knocked on Beccy's door and entered. Beccy, bathed and dressed only in a slip, was silhouetted against the light from the window. She was leaning forward and brushing her hair which hung as a lustrous black sheen in front of her. The fashion since the war had been to have 'bobbed' hair which suited Bernadette's russet waves, but Beccy had kept hers long. She sat on a chair, Bernadette took the brush and smoothed down the raven strands.

"Very special engagement tonight, Beccy," said Bernadette. "Expecting to dine with two people and I am fairly certain we shall be invited afterwards to see a Poussin." As she continued to brush the hair she looked downward over Beccy's head and noticed her small pointed breasts. "Are you a virgin?" she asked.

Beccy rose from the chair and looked out onto the Konstanzer below where some youths in grey flannels and white shirts were parading and carrying banners. The women had been in Berlin only half a day and it seemed as though most of the population was in some sort of uniform. Swastikas hung from many shop fronts and loud speakers were being erected on telegraph poles.

Beccy had been associated with Bernadette for some eighteen months and this was the first occasion she felt any kind of embarrassment. Bernadette felt Beccy's unease, went to the window and looked down at the parade in the street below. She put her hand on Beccy's shoulder.

"Sorry. Please forgive me," she said, quietly.

At dinner that night the women looked ravishing. Bernadette wore a bottle-green velvet gown with a black waistcoat. She radiated maturity and confidence, and her genial smile greeted the male escorts, one of whom was her son. Beccy was dressed in a long sheath of black satin. She looked very pale and slightly apprehensive. Why hadn't Bernadette mentioned her son was to be present, she wondered.

The meal began rather ponderously and did not thaw out until it was discovered that both George and Beccy spoke German fluently. By the approach of the sweets trolley plans had been made to move on to a house in the suburbs for a private viewing. They were met at the hotel door by a chauffeur and three of them sat in the rear compartment of the Packard limousine. George had politely excused himself and said he hoped to see them all again soon.

They drove for what seemed only a very short distance. The sound of wheels over gravel gave the women notice of their destination. They were ushered into a palatial house and offered coffee. Bernadette was the epitome of unhurried patience. Beccy struggled to maintain her poise. And then their host revealed his picture. Bernadette inspected it closely. It was beautifully lighted and displayed. Beccy had expected it to be larger. The party sat again and discussed generalities.

Beccy was surprised to see the time showing nearly midnight and had a further shock when George was announced. After the murmuring of general thanks they left their host having made arrangements to see the picture next day, in daylight. The chauffeur escorted George, Beccy and his mother back to the Glockner where George took his leave.

"But I had no idea he was to be there," said Bernadette. "He has a flat in Berlin, but I honestly did not know he was in residence. I told him in a letter of our latest project and I suppose he thought it would be exciting to meet us unexpectedly."

And as if that were sufficient explanation she thanked Beccy for her support, laid plans for tomorrow's meeting and bid her goodnight.

Beccy lay long awake. She was strangely disturbed. The language had returned so easily to her and she had conversed with George and the others as a native speaker. Which, on reflection, gave her the shock of realising she was literally a native. Her thoughts flew to her father. She could see his pale face as he echoed the word "Berlin." She saw George appear from nowhere and embrace his mother as though it were the most natural thing in the world to meet at a dinner party in Berlin. She did not think she could have come to the city as a small child, certainly had no memories of it. George and Bernadette and Daddy and Poussin and Poussin and Daddy and George and George. It was worse than trying to count sheep.

By early daylight the picture looked even more lovely. Bernadette gave it authentication, signed the appropriate documents and telephoned a London address. The two women supervised the picture's carcassing for freight passage and then returned to the Glockner. They had only an hour for hurried shopping as they had to be at the airport at midday. George had arranged to see them off and to help with the luggage. The picture travelled with them and at Paris they made no overnight stop. At Croydon the documents were duly presented, the import certificate endorsed, and they were on their way by taxi to an address in Kenwood. Here the picture had reached its destination. The women were invited into the gallery and the strings and wrappings were removed from the parcel. The Poussin was tried in several locations and when at last it was resolved they all stood in admiration. Congratulations were offered and accepted and Bernadette and Beccy left for home.

Chapter Eighteen

Beccy was dropped off with her hand luggage at Hampstead Road with instructions to contact St. John's Wood by telephone the day after tomorrow.

Tom opened the door for her with an open-arms greeting. Leo was tidying the workplace and Rachel was with Joe in the kitchen. Supper was a joyous occasion that evening, and afterwards Beccy distributed the small presents she had brought for them all. A cigar box which contained small portions of exotic cheese was for her father and a carved wooden platter, inscribed with the words *"Gib Uns Heute Unser Taglich Brot"* was for Rachel. She had neckties, which would have been considered too gaudy for the English market for the menfolk. Joseph and Tom chose theirs and left five others for Robert Moser and the work-hands to have the following day.

After supper, when Leo had listened carefully to all the details of Beccy's excursion, and when the others had left the room to admire Tom's new decor for the workroom, he took his unopened box of cheeses and pushed it into the hob of the stove. It was a stupid and irrational action he knew and for the first time in his life he seemed to be beside himself. Emotionally, he had to destroy the cheeses because he thought they formed a link, albeit ephemerally with a past he had long dismissed as forbidden. He was shaking and pale when Rachel returned to the kitchen. She held him tight until he stopped trembling, then she took the wooden platter from his hand, dusted it on her apron and propped it up on the dresser.

"Those days are gone for ever dear boy," she whispered, "kiss me."

Chapter Nineteen

Tom walked in the park with Beccy later that evening. Hesitatingly, he spoke of his love.

"Would you consider marrying me?"

Beccy knew Tom to be a dear, dear boy and would have considered it patronising to say so. She had never known such a generous, unselfish, kind-hearted person. That made it all the more difficult for her. She had always cherished their mutual affection, had even taken it for granted. And if he had asked her, even a month ago, she might have agreed to an engagement. And now, since Berlin, she had changed. Certainly George had given her no special encouragement, but she had been so stirred by his natural charm and hoped their friendship would develop. Although, to be honest, she did not know whether George had any special feeling for her. She struggled to form an answer for Tom. She felt as if she were choking. Through a constricted throat that neither of them recognised, she replied.

"I don't suppose you will ever forgive me. I cannot speak about marriage yet."

Tom asked for no explanation. He was a very patient man. They wheeled in their tracks and walked back to Beccy's house. Tom did not put in an appearance at Hampstead Road the following day. But on the day after he caught Beccy just as she was hurrying out for St. John's Wood. He had something important to tell her. He had enrolled in the International Brigade. Beccy stood aghast. He was the least bellicose man she could imagine. She knew of his political conviction, of course, from their Sunday School days, but had not realised he could be so utterly committed. Perhaps she should have realised. She assumed he had fully discussed the matter at home and learned that Eric and Dot had, probably grudgingly, accepted his viewpoint. Neither Beccy or Tom could delay. Tom dashed in to say farewell to his favourite family after watching Beccy walk quickly away toward Regent's Park. She turned once and waved.

He was to be greatly missed from the Hampstead Road premises which he had been so instrumental in improving. Rachel showed more apparent concern than anyone. She was full of questioning.

"Why did you? Could your application be rescinded? But you don't have to go yet". She hugged him hard, and added: "Take great care! You must look out for yourself." He shook hands with Leo and Robert and the workmen. Rachel hugged him again. "Please write if you can," she said.

They all watched him leave.

He wrote within a week, from Liverpool, to say he was embarking on a steamship for a destination in Morocco.

Chapter Twenty

Before Tom had left, he had decorated and improved the semi-basement at Hampstead Road which Robert Moser had been able to purchase. For the first time in their lives the Radstones had a living room separate from a kitchen.

One of the rooms in this new accommodation was used as a store for tailoring materials; this relieved the pressure on the workroom. With Robert's direction and Leo's management the business progressed steadily. Robert would have preferred a less conservative cut to the suit designs but had to agree that Leo gave his clientele what they wanted. Robert had ideas for opening a new branch of his business where his preferred designs would be produced.

Joseph was progressing steadily with his craft at the School of Furniture Design. After being taught to make internal and external patterns for the bodies of violins, he had been introduced to some of the finer points. He had made up laminates for purflin and had succeeded with several neck scrolls. It was conceded that many attempts had found their way into the scrap bin but he eventually became competent. He learned that when a good scroll could be carved the art and craft of the luthier was in reach.

By the midsummer of 1937 Beccy received a letter from Tom who had just arrived in mainland Spain. He had very little to report. He was well. He sent his love to all, especially to her. And would she write to him? Now that Beccy had an address to reach Tom she wrote to him straight away. She gave him all the latest developments at home and said how much they all enjoyed the extra accommodation and how indebted they were to him for his work. Then she wrote as delicately as she could about their last conversation, which she found exceedingly difficult to pen.

Beccy cycled back to the East End that Sunday to see Eric and Dot, and when the Club closed she went back with them to their house. They had received their first letter from Tom who considered he was taking part in a 'just' war. Eric and Dot hardly knew what to make of it; they were in a very sombre mood. Eric had recently added to his list of responsibilities by trying, as an agent, to promote sales of the 'Left Book Club.' He was a prolific and discerning reader, he studied subjects thoroughly and endeavoured to reach conclusions, albeit tentatively. And now, having Tom in the front line, as it were, had tempered his opinion.

The Fishers were courteous and considerate as ever. They wanted to hear all Beccy's news, especially from her recent visit to Germany. Dot had visited The Black Forest several times and had, on one occasion, taken a party of girls from her school on a summer excursion. It seemed to Beccy to be ages ago since Dot had invited her to join the party to see 'Lady Precious Stream' at The Open Air Theatre and how difficult she had found it subsequently to call Mrs. Fisher 'Dot.'

Dot thought how mature and composed Beccy had become. Always a resourceful girl she remembered, but now metamorphosed into a woman of accomplishment and vision. But Dot was very preoccupied, her only son with the Brigade. She knew of his feelings for Beccy, though he had been reticent of expression. And here was Beccy, their favourite student; how could they but love her.

Chapter Twenty-One

Beccy was with Bernadette at her apartment in St. John's Wood. They discussed the Berlin project and, after studying the financial accounts, agreed it had been a total success. A cheque had been received for the transaction and when all expenses for travelling and accommodation had been deducted, there remained a credit in the account of more than three hundred pounds. Beccy was amazed that such a sum could accrue in a week of easy living and good companionship, but she then realised the finances had to be weighed over a longer period. Beccy received ten per cent of the profit and paid thirty pounds into her bank account, opened a year ago and from which she had made no withdrawal.

The women had to make plans for another visit to Dublin. Artefacts were leaving the continent regularly and in greater volume now than Bernadette could remember. The Free State appeared to make insatiable demands upon the market; and she was their invaluable courier. Beccy stood in some awe of Bernadette's expertise and drive, but was a very able and willing student. She learned, among other things, that in this business speed of decision was of the essence.

Their journeys to Dublin soon became regular and quite commonplace. George was invariably present, which delighted Beccy. There was a magnetism about him which she could not accurately define. His nearness affected her strongly and she discovered new feelings which she thought should be restrained. This was a novel experience for Beccy. Her affectionate nature had, in the past, adequately matched her strength of friendship. But when George was near her all the simple and recognised reactions seemed to take on a behaviour of their own volition. Beccy forced her mind to the business in hand. George had recently helped his mother negotiate a transaction involving a pair of rare Dresden vases. The precious vases were safe, at the present, in a Berlin vault. And upon this information the women formed their plans for their next visit to Germany.

They remained for several nights in Paris, and although their absence had been for only six months the differences to be seen were quite remarkable. The Latin Quarter, which Beccy loved to visit was much as usual, but there were signs of ugly brick-built air-raid shelters being erected. As in England, many people thought war would not actually come about, and there appeared to be a rather dilettante preparedness except that most French men spoke of the 'invincibility of the Maginot Line.'

The air-crew of the Deutsche Luft Hansa taking them on to Berlin were cheerful and charming. The flight was smooth and when they landed George was there to meet them. If he was a little more sombre than usual it did not detract from the greeting he offered his mother and Beccy. She was not sure whether her feet had firmly touched down when George gave her a big hug. He saw them to their hotel and arranged to meet them again in the evening.

The women's routine of negotiations seemed to fall into a pattern usually involving an informal dinner party and sometimes a soirée of sorts; on this occasion a visit to a night club. The city itself, always cheerful with an ambience of "cockney" demeanour, appeared to be rather less buoyant than on their earlier visit. But if the rumours of war were rumbling outside, in the night-club the scene was riotous and brash, with raucous hilarity. Occasionally a stand-up comedian shot a telling barb, especially mimicking the English Prime Minister, Chamberlain, and his bowler-hatted aides, but these were not the favoured jokes and were met with less than wild acclaim. Even some Jewish jokes fell flat, almost as though they had either already been played out, or they left a risqué feeling of treading on thin ice. But this was inside the club. George escorted the women back to their hotel in the small hours and the eerie silence of the city evoked a sense of foreboding.

On the day they had left London Rachel had walked through Regent's Park with Beccy and they had sat at the lakeside for a few minutes. Rachel opened a subject she had never mentioned before. She told Beccy of her parents. Her father had been lost at the battle of Somme, presumed dead; no body had been found. Her mother had died soon after and had been buried in a north Berlin cemetery. She had no other details. If the opportunity arose would Beccy consider looking for her grandmother's grave? Beccy affirmed she would try, time permitting, and neither women harboured any realistic hope of achievement.

Early on this bright spring morning in Berlin, of 1938, when Bernadette had departed alone to collect an unframed pencil sketch by Turner, Beccy set out from the Glockner hotel by taxi to the Friedhof. In the attached chapel of remembrance an assistant courteously helped Beccy as best she could from the sparse details. All she had was 'Lotte Beatrix Bach died 1918' and a pencilled note which said her husband's name might be added to the headstone: 'Albricht Bach - soldier.' The index of names, kept neatly in chests of drawers, was thoroughly searched, but the name could not be found.

The helpful assistant seemed to understand why there were so few details and suggested Beccy should continue her search at a small cemetery off Landsberger Allee. She even volunteered to telephone her imminent arrival. Beccy accepted the offer gratefully and made her way by taxi toward the east of Berlin, found the Friedhof and made enquiries. Yes, the name had been forwarded and a search had been made to no avail. She was shown the appropriate list meticulously kept in alphabetical order. She was directed to yet another cemetery and here met with the same result. She was advised to make an appointment at the Central Record Office where she should receive a definitive result. She took a taxi to the Record Office and duly made her enquiry. She was informed that it might take several days to uncover the information. They asked for her London address, took a search fee and promised to forward any findings. And there, feeling frustrated and, rather weary, Beccy had to leave the matter.

Chapter Twenty-Two

The following morning Bernadette left the Turner sketch at the hotel and the two women set off in search of the Dresden vases. George had some specialisation in porcelain and he was to be involved in the exercise. The weather was glorious; crocuses grew in profusion in Victoria Park and, as the two women walked lightly together, they could have been taken for mother and daughter. Bernadette had indeed aspirations in this direction. She had grown very fond of her protégée, enjoyed her company and was especially observant of her when George was present. Like many parents, she had unspoken hopes for her offspring. She thought they looked well together, loved to see them discussing seriously the current business and particularly admired their total and unconscious multi-lingual ability. This was not only a great boon to her international dealings but also seemed to forge a strong link between them.

They were all to meet, they understood, an elderly Jewish woman who had come by the vases many years ago. She now lived very quietly on her own. George had agreed to the women going on ahead. They were dressed simply as suited the occasion. Bernadette wore a pale-green tailored two-piece suit and Beccy caught the atmosphere of a sunny Spring morning with a short floral dress. They were met at the door of a rather run-down block of flats by a janitor who directed them up the stone steps to a first-floor apartment. Frau Hugel was prepared and waiting for them. Quite simply she was offering the vases for sale to help her son, daughter-in-law and grandchildren emigrate to America. She needed as much money as she could raise and there was a great urgency about the matter.

Beccy was privy to the maximum figure which Bernadette had been authorised to offer and was mildly surprised, although she showed no reaction, when Bernadette stated the probability of a considerably lower amount. The vases looked plain, small and rather cold but she was pretty sure they were genuine. Bernadette addressed her remark to Frau Hugel.

"Would you have any objection to my son inspecting the vases?"

On the receipt of positive affirmation Beccy left the apartment and waited in the street below for George, whom she had arranged to meet half an hour after the agreed appointment time with Frau Hugel. He was certainly good looking, she thought, with his boyish stride and cheerful grin as he brushed Beccy's cheek with a perfunctory kiss.

"Before we go in I want to ask you to offer the maximum amount if you decide to have the vases. Please." She explained her reason for this request. George looked vaguely mystified but he seemed never to engage in argument.

"Mother arranges the deal," he said.

When they entered the flat Bernadette was having a cup of coffee, and she looked up at the youngsters in a motherly way. Frau Hugel seemed quite surprised at George's youthfulness. He handled the vases with a delicacy that belied his offhand, debonair manner. He took them to the window and held them to the light. He smoothed the porcelain against his face. He stood them on a table and regarded them as a pair; and finally he upturned them and recorded their provenance. They were genuine without doubt, and better still Meissen and in pristine condition.

He acknowledged all his findings openly to the women. Bernadette restated her first offer. Frau Hugel looked ill and terribly old, but she summoned the courage to refuse. They left her then with a promise to return by noon when they hoped, after further discussion, to bring her a more generous offer. Back at the Glockner Bernadette and George were engaged in intimate conversation. After half an hour had elapsed she returned to the lounge and made a telephone call to London. She then informed George and Beccy that they should retrace their steps to Frau Hugel's after visiting the bank.

George made a cash transaction while Beccy waited outside the bank in the sunshine. Still they had three-quarters of an hour to spare before their appointment. Beccy suggested arriving early to surprise Frau Hugel with the good news, but George felt quite sure that surprises, even nice ones, were not called for at the moment.

Just on mid-day they were met by Frau Hugel's son who was accompanied by a friend, introduced as a solicitor, to witness the deal. And now the conditions had been changed. He would not authorise the deal until, in addition to the agreed amount of payment, they were given tickets for the rail journey to Bremen and single liner tickets to New York for two adults and two children. Beccy was invited to remain with Frau Hugel while George hurried away to see if he could arrange the business. It was three hours before he returned; the women had learned each other's life story. He looked totally unperturbed and was able to place the travel tickets and the cash into the hands of Frau Hugel. What seemed, to Beccy, to be a fabulous amount of money was accepted and a prepared receipt was signed.

While George and Frau Hugel's son packed the vases into a cardboard box, liberally stuffed with rag and newspaper, Beccy continued quietly talking with the grandmother. The box was finally tied with rough sisal string which served as a handy grip. Its inconspicuous appearance was sufficient camouflage for a collector's item of rare porcelain. They made their farewells, and Beccy found herself very moved with the dignity of the mother and son.

Outside, the afternoon sun had sunk below the tree line; there was a promise of early frost in the air. Beccy was glad to wear George's raincoat over her light dress. They retraced their steps through the park as the shadows lengthened. They were to take the vases to George's accommodation. Beccy had not been there before and was intrigued to see he lived in a Corbusier-style block. But on entering the flat she was surprised at the decor, the positioning of his classical furniture and the beautifully arranged collection of objets d'art. Then she wondered why she should be surprised. It was all part of a pattern; George's upbringing, comparative wealth, and the life-chances he had been offered. She had not really seen him before without his mother and in his own realm, as it were, and she liked what she saw. The debonair and rather suave young graduate seemed to change, with the closing of his apartment door, into a more mature, quietly considerate person.

The charm was still apparent but it was modified; he reflected his surroundings and his surroundings formed a warm reflective backcloth to his character. Beccy had divested herself of his raincoat and was glad to feel the general warmth of the underfloor central heating. She wandered around the flat openly inspecting the artefacts while he was in the kitchenette brewing tea.

"Stay for supper," he called. "A few friends should be joining us."

He was a most considerate host. He answered all Beccy's questions about his belongings; their dates and origins; which were of greatest intrinsic value; and about some items, like a simple collection of pebbles he had collected as a boy from Galway that were irreplaceable. They unpacked the Dresden vases with great care and placed them on a fairly high shelf above a bookcase. The apartment was clean and smelled fragrant. George explained that he had the services of a regular housekeeper who would be returning any minute now to prepare an evening meal. How the time had flown!

By seven, two guests arrived; a tall man with blonde hair, introduced simply as Hans who bent over Beccy's hand, almost clicked his heels and caused a ripple of simple laughter. He was escorting a young lady of Beccy's age named Claudette, also blonde. She was rather shy and very beautiful. Hans told them that Rikard had sent double apologies: first because he would not be able to be with them this evening and secondly for the deplorably short notice. His reasons were given, and it was added that he was especially sorry not to meet Rebecca. Beccy was becoming used to surprises, but now her expression showed only mutual disappointment.

They were a very congenial small party; Frau Behrn had prepared and served an exquisitely cooked meal of simple ingredients and George had opened a bottle of chilled white wine. Claudette and Hans were soon to be married and much of the conversation turned upon their preparations, where they lived and consideration of their general prospects. At the supper table the Austrian Anschluss was not mentioned even though the wireless and papers were full of the news. In the street it seemed to be an all-pervading topic.

By nine-thirty Frau Behrn left; George made coffee which they drank with liqueur and the four of them settled replete and congenial into quiet conversation. It had gone eleven when Hans and Claudette decided to leave; could they see Beccy back to the Glockner? they asked. George asked her to stay and thanked them for their kindness as they took their leave.

When they had gone, George placed the vases on to a coffee table and arranged the light from the standard lamp to shine directly on to them. He sat on a chaise- longue close to Beccy and as he looked up, the porcelain appeared translucent.

"Porcelain needs warming," he said, and he carefully reached forward and gave a vase to Beccy. She held it close, in both hands, and imagined its colour responded to her warmth. It was a most beautiful object. George ran his fingertips delicately around the contours of the vase on the nearby table, then traced its vertical lines while keeping one eye closed. He brought the vase slowly toward his body. With the gracefulness of a spider in its web he took the hem of Beccy's skirt, slid the porcelain with gossamer lightness on to her thighs and let the material of the thin dress caress the vase. Beccy remained motionless and silent, continuing to regard the vase in her hands. She felt as though her chest was on fire and would burst. Her stomach contracted; her head was swimming. Was she affronted or just bewildered? Despite this confusion of mind she remained motionless, her slender fingers angled toward the light. She was holding the vase too tightly; her knuckles showed white.

After a timeless interval, she placed the vase, with exaggerated calm, on to the coffee table. Withdrawing the other one she put it carefully beside its twin, then turned slowly and deliberately toward George. She thought he looked uncertain for once as he imploringly searched her eyes. From the hallway came the half-muffled sound of the grandfather clock. The two young people were frozen in tableau as it slowly boomed its final message of the day. Only then did they relax. Beccy reached forward and with extended fingertips traced the profile of his forehead. George slid his hands around her waist and kissed her pale, serious face. The shadow cast by the vases enveloped their happiness.

Very early the following morning George and Beccy returned to the Glockner. Tenderly kissing her, he left her then, arranging to call at ten o'clock. Beccy had breakfast with Bernadette who looked wonderingly at the girl's pleasant face.

"We shall have to be quick" she said. "George will be here at ten."

Exactly on time he arrived and escorted the women with their luggage to the aerodrome.

"When shall I see you again?" he asked.

His mother said she would be in Dublin in the summer. Beccy smiled shyly and whispered in his ear.

"I hope it's much sooner than that."

"I have to stay in Berlin for a while. I will see you as soon as possible," he said.

All three of them stood in a tight huddle of affection. It was a cherished moment for them. As they walked across the tarmac to the waiting aeroplane George transferred a parcel to Beccy.

"Protect this with your life," he laughed.

"Am I worth all that amount?" she said, as she slipped the sisal loop over her hand.

Chapter Twenty-Three

Their journey home was simple. For once they had not been asked to declare anything in Paris or at Croydon where they landed as darkness fell. They travelled on directly to St. John's Wood and as Beccy saw Bernadette safely ensconced she handed her the precious parcel. As she had not let it go since George had given it to her in Berlin her hand was now quite red and sore from the friction of the sisal handle. She was glad, at last, to slip it off.

"Protect this with your life" she mimicked, and they both laughed.

"Good night dear girl. Off you go now. Thank you for all your help."

Beccy took the taxi on to Hampstead Road, and there, like old times, Thomas Fisher was the first to greet her. Dear Tom! He appeared to be bigger than when she had last seen him. Here he was, fresh from an escapade in Spain which she was eager to learn about. She could hardly believe Tom had been invalided out of the Brigade. True he had received a shoulder wound, but he seemed to be fully recovered, and she was very pleased he had decided not to return to the front. Tom's experience in Spain had been chaotic and unorganised and he was not at all sure whether or not *his* bullet had come from 'friendly fire.'

They all enjoyed a very special evening together. The premises, now extended to two floors, had made a great deal of difference to their lives. Beccy contributed generously to the family budget and the business was flourishing. Robert Moser had been good at getting orders in the hard times of the slump industry, but now it seemed he could not put a foot wrong. And as the days lengthened into summer a large order for military uniforms was received.

This second half of the year brought further changes to the Radstone household. Leo had charge of the whole business as it affected the premises at Hampstead Road, and by arrangement with Robert had been made a partner in the firm.

Robert was a generous man of strong principles. At the time of his first meeting with Leo he had been courting Clarence Nagel. It was, in fact, through Clarence that Leo and he had first met. Clarence had lived above the Radstones' when they were in the East End, had befriended Beccy, and had introduced customers to Rachel's dressmaking. Whether Robert had spent too much time thinking of business and had not sufficiently considered Clarence was a moot point. Clarence had had only one day a week off from domestic employment and it transpired that as Robert's business grew they had found less time for each other. By mutual consent they had annulled their engagement. Clarence obtained a housekeeper's position in a large country house in Buckinghamshire and Robert had given his undivided attention to his business. He was resolved to be a success and with a determined singleness of mind pursued the trade he understood so well. He relied entirely upon Leo's expertise in cutting and fitting while he devoted most of his time to obtaining new orders. And this left him with very little time for much socialising or for female company.

In the late Autumn of 1938 Robert was again able to enlarge the premises. He had negotiated for, and then purchased, the upper two storeys at Hampstead Road. The whole of this large house was now his, freehold, and it was at this point in his career that he offered Leo a partnership in the firm. He knew that Leo could not manage to raise a premium but had calculated that his work was sound and as the business expanded he had become its indispensable main-stay. He also knew, better than anyone, that with the Radstones you traded on their utmost goodwill and loyalty.

Leo was to receive dividends and the financial arrangement was amicably concluded. Tom Fisher took charge of the alterations to the property and was eventually employed as general factotum. There were sewing machines of many kinds, electric presses and irons to be maintained and the new boiler to be installed for central heating and hot water. Robert believed he could not have a better staff and left them to get on with their work while he did his; which was to get orders and arrange for the continuous supply of materials, and, as has already been noted, he accomplished this with efficiency.

Chapter Twenty-Four

In February of 1939 Beccy made another foray into Germany. Again she travelled by air, accompanied by Bernadette, and again they stayed for a few days in Paris. Beccy's colloquial French was now completely fluent and she felt as confident in France as she did in Germany. Being a natural linguist, she thought and spoke in whichever language presented itself.

She had not received a reply from the Central Record Office in Berlin regarding the location of her grandmother's grave and she resolved to make further enquiries if time permitted. She also longed to be with George. He disappeared unaccountably for long periods and Bernadette was usually unable to give Beccy any information as to his whereabouts. She had last seen him in Dublin where she enjoyed a short holiday there at the New Year. She had not heard from him since. Not a post card or a 'phone call. Bernadette felt strongly they would see him in Berlin.

Artefacts were reasonably easy to come by now and the market was saturated with would-be buyers. Great ingenuity was used sometimes to circumvent the exchange of cash. Stocks were transferred, overseas property was secured, goods were bartered. On this occasion the women had to collect what Bernadette deemed to be little more than bric-a-brac. They did not consider themselves to be expert in this field but it was such an easy, lucrative market, they felt they could not go far wrong. The most complicated part of the transaction was passing through customs. The authorities were meticulous, and a deal of time was used in specifying their declarations.

For Beccy it was a drear and unhappy time. She was not able either to visit the Record Office in Berlin, nor to make another personal search in the grave-yard files. The friendly atmosphere that had characterised Berlin for her on previous occasions had vanished, the weather was atrocious and she did not see George. She felt unutterably miserable. Bernadette had never been so pressurised with work; she too, would have enjoyed George's company, and she felt unable to alleviate Beccy's distress. She, quite simply, did not know where he was.

When the women returned to London and learned that he was neither there nor in Dublin they became considerably alarmed. Beccy went home low in spirit and her family, always supportive, did their best to understand and comfort her.

When she returned to St. John's Wood two days later Bernadette greeted her with a hug. The women were almost inseparable now but, in her anxiety, Beccy shrugged off the greeting. Bernadette had not been able to discover anything of George's whereabouts.

"I contacted a friend at the Home Office the day we got home," she said. "He could tell me nothing of him at all. Suggested I contact Berlin. I told him we had visited George's address there, to no avail."

"But we must enquire at the Embassy," said Beccy. "They must be able to tell us something."

In a mood of near desperation Bernadette contacted the Irish Ambassador. From this source Bernadette received the terse message "Your son is incommunicado." The Embassy spokesman was unwilling or unable to offer any other information. There the matter had to rest.

Beccy was frantic with anxiety and this reduced Bernadette to tears. Both women felt emotionally exhausted and for a moment clung to each other in silence. Beccy gradually became more irreconcilable and uncharacteristically morose.

Through the months of June and July she felt the marked contrast between London and Berlin more sharply than ever. Apart from the intellectuals and the more thinking members of the general public the mood during this hot summer in London was of optimism and almost reckless gaiety. The older people felt that at least they were more prepared for war than in 1914. The younger adults were far from pessimistic. They showed signs of wishing to 'get on with it,' to defeat Hitler and to get back to normal. The children were excited and were learning about plans for their evacuation to the country. Many of the children did not want to leave London, but the majority got used to the idea of its inevitability. The only parents to be evacuated were those accompanying babies; for the great majority, the families were going to be split up.

Despite some trepidation caused by the rapid circulation of scare-stories, London this summer, remained its usual boisterous, optimistic self. The open-air swimming baths had never been so well-patronised and the yells and delighted squeals of the children splashing and playing in the water gave the lie to any augury of ominousness. And Beccy could contrast this only with the sombre seriousness of her last view of Berlin.

Chapter Twenty-Five

On the day war was declared against Germany in September 1939, Robert Moser delivered to Leo an order for uniforms for the Women's Auxiliary Air Force. They were to make a trial batch of tunics and skirts in blue-grey serge. The material received was of good quality and Leo set about the task immediately. He was ordered to make a dozen sets in six sizes. He enlisted Rachel's help and, rather more reluctantly, Beccy's.

Both women acquiesced, helped with stitching and eventually the modelling. They paraded around the workroom together and it was the first time they had seen Beccy laugh for a long while. Neither women had the right colour stockings to match the outfits so decided to be bare-legged. Neither did they have the correct shirts, so wearing only tunic and skirt, and with no shoes, walked, marched, even grotesquely swaggered around the workshop. At last the ice was broken and Leo and Robert, Rachel and Beccy enjoyed the moment. Small adjustments, tacks and chalk marks were made to the uniforms and the women left to change back into their own clothes. Gradually the workshop settled down again to complete the order. It had been a small but happy event which Beccy recalled as being another mile-stone in her career.

She returned to St. John's Wood where she now spent most of her time. Their import orders had dried up and she was engaged in preparing the accounts for the auditors. Bernadette was like a ship without a rudder. For all her worldliness, maturity and good connections she felt overawed by the sheer weight of current affairs. In sharper tones than usual, one afternoon, she said, "I am leaving for Dublin and closing this apartment for the duration." She could not bear to say 'for the possible duration of this ridiculous war.' "And Beccy, dear, I want you to come with me."

Beccy remained silent.

"Your family will be all right here, but if you wish to bring your mother and father they will be welcome."

She knew they would never leave the business, but she went on "I have plenty of accommodation in Ireland. You must be with me Beccy, you must not leave me." Bernadette was nearly shouting now "I insist on your accompanying me and we shall leave as soon as the arrangement for the sale of this property has been settled."

Beccy looking unresponsive.

"Go and tell your family what we intend to do." Bernadette trailed off weakly as though all her considerable resources had suddenly failed. She was sobbing quietly. In what seemed to be a reversal of roles Beccy put her arms around Bernadette and held her tightly until she was calm. She could not at the moment say a word. But in the silence that followed she asked Bernadette if she had heard from George. Bernadette struggled to regain her equilibrium and between gasps said something about "the futility of it all." Beccy resolved not to mention his name to her again. After a few moments Bernadette regained some of her composure and withdrew.

Left alone, it was Beccy's turn to feel bewildered and drained. Bernadette would not refer to her son. Whenever his name was mentioned she became distraught and emotional and could not face Beccy. Beccy stood motionless, looking from the bay window which gave on to the park. It was a sombre scene. Many of the flower beds had not been replanted and a profusion of sandbags in various stages of preparation lay around the untidy barrage-balloon site. Eventually she dragged herself back to the accounts book and through sheer discipline settled to the work. She made herself some tea for refreshment and quite assumed Bernadette would be down to join her. But she was asleep on her bed when Beccy looked in to see her at eight o'clock.

"I'm going now," she whispered,

"See you tomorrow at nine." Bernadette opened her eyes and reached for Beccy's hand.

The following morning Bernadette was up, breakfast had been cleared away (she no longer employed a maid,) when Beccy came in using her own key. To all intents and purposes Bernadette sounded normal. She looked vaguely paler, had obviously been suffering from stress, but reacted to Beccy's appearance with usual pleasure and intimacy. She wished to apologise for breaking down yesterday. Beccy hugged her.

"I cannot come with you," she said.

"Of course not," whispered Bernadette.

They then discovered there were many things to do in a hurry. Bernadette did not wish to give Beccy the responsibility for tidying up her affairs at St. John's Wood. She would leave, she repeated, only when all the arrangements had been made. Meanwhile Beccy was to continue treating the apartment as her own. Her salary would continue, naturally, until Bernadette was ensconced in Dublin. And even then there might be a chance of continuing with their business.

The tailoring business of Moser and Radstone was flourishing and Rachel was as content as she had ever been. Joseph had discontinued his apprenticeship at the outbreak of war and was now working at the De Havilland's aircraft factory, north of London. Thomas Fisher remained as solid an anchor man at Hampstead Road as the proprietors could wish for.

Chapter Twenty-Six

Through the good offices of Robert Moser, Bernadette finally sold her premises, in the January of 1940, to the military authorities. They had made the purchase because they needed large apartments in St. John's Wood for billeting purposes. Most of the neighbouring houses had been commandeered.

A few evenings before Bernadette was finally to remove to Dublin she was invited to supper at Hampstead Road. Joseph was not present, he had lodgings in Hertfordshire; Tom Fisher discreetly went to visit his parents in the East End, and Robert had left as usual at about six o'clock. The little party was gentle and sympathetic to the prevailing mood. Rachel was a motherly yet discreet hostess and Leo was totally himself, as usual, except that he was dressed for the occasion. That is to say, he wore a longue suit, collar and tie. Bernadette had not visited before, although she had been closely associated with Beccy for more than three years. She had heard all about the members of the enterprise and thought she had formed a fair picture; but she was very agreeably surprised and, for a person who had seen so much of the world, impressed. The house did smell fairly strongly of serge-wool and cottons and linen, but it was far from being unpleasant. The stairs from the upper hall which led down to the parlour were rather poorly illuminated but the contrast on entering the room was all the more noticeable. The large table was already laid and the utensils appeared simple and welcoming. No preparatory drink was offered and when the four of them were ready to sit the candles were lit, and the electric light extinguished. It was a most graceful repast. There was no strain felt in any relationship.

They were living through very difficult times and usually were so busy they had little time for reflection. Bernadette spoke freely and was relieved to relate to trustworthy ears. Rachel and Leo were the souls of discretion. Their background offered no shelter to innuendo or gossip and they, in turn, were agreeably pleased with Mrs. Lampard about whom they had heard so much. For this one evening it was as though they were members of the same family. Bernadette greatly appreciated the intimacy of their company and was restored to more equanimity than she had known for some months. She had a taxi home and asked Beccy to call in the morning. She had only three days left in the old apartment and she wanted to tie up the last few outstanding threads of business.

In the morning Beccy was at St. John's Wood. Much of the furniture had been removed and there was a dismal atmosphere of muskiness as some of the carpets had been lifted. But today, Bernadette was serious and confidently in command; much as she used to be. The auditors' report had been received and the business, so far as London was concerned, was wound up. Bernadette hoped to be able to continue in Dublin, but everything in the art-dealers' market was as closed now as it had been burgeoning for the past few years.

Now there were much more serious events to consider. Bernadette had applied for, and had been accepted into, the diplomatic branch of the Eire Civil Service, and was to take up her post the following week. She knew Beccy would not join her in Ireland and she was anxious to know what she would do. Beccy had no plans. There was now full employment; jobs were plentiful, especially in engineering. Teaching posts were, in the main, considered not to be reserved occupations. Consequently there were many vacancies in the profession, especially for languages. She could easily have applied for a position in a school but had not seriously considered the option. So far as Bernadette could elicit Beccy had not fully realised the implication of her being unemployed, and she did not want her to be forcibly directed into unsuitable work.

Despite the women's close association Bernadette suddenly realised how little she knew of Beccy. At last night's supper she had been so mature, natural, unaffected and accommodating and now she saw standing before her a young lady, vulnerable through her transparent honesty. Bernadette had to summon all her resourcefulness in tact and understanding now she felt overwhelmingly Beccy to be her responsibility.

"You are a wonderful linguist; have you thought about joining the Services as an interpreter?" She guessed, of course, that no such thing had crossed her mind. "They run training classes in languages, but the products they turn out are pretty pitiful. You would be welcomed with open arms as an instructor, or you might find a post in active service." Bernadette felt she was waffling now, and Beccy had made no response.

They made some coffee and Bernadette tried to hedge around the subject again. At last she said: "I cannot leave you until I know you have made some definite plans for the future." Then she realised how ridiculous that had sounded and she giggled;

Beccy joined in and presently they collapsed with the exhaustion of laughing. "O! Pompous," shrieked Bernadette, and then hardly moving her lips, whispered: "Dear, dear child."

Chapter Twenty-Seven

Beccy saw Bernadette off from Paddington. It was not quite the chilling departure Bernadette had feared. She had left it as late as the taxi ride to the station to tell Beccy she had mentioned her name to a senior officer in the Air Force and hoped she did not mind. She knew of the crying need for linguists in the Forces, and Beccy's welfare was uppermost in her mind. Beccy did not know at this moment whether she minded or not and nodded only as an indication that she had heard.

She took a taxi from Paddington intending to return home, but decided on the spur of the moment to call on the Fishers in the East End. Dot Fisher was at home. She had been evacuated with the children to Bedfordshire, but had returned to the Commercial Road after only three months. Many of the evacuated children, too, had come back to London, especially those of secondary age. Organising some kind of schooling posed great problems for the authorities, the teachers and the children themselves. The old school buildings were condemned as being largely unfit for use in war time and had no air-raid shelters. Many of the city's buildings were three-storied and where possible the ground floor only was adapted for some kind of emergency education. The staircases were fitted with padlocked iron gates. They could not be bricked off because access to the roof had to be maintained in case of fire from incendiary bombs.

Dot clasped Beccy in her arms as though she would never let her go. Then for a second they smiled at each other. Then they both burst out laughing together. They had so much to catch up on. Eric's Sunday Club had been totally disbanded. Hooliganism had turned to vandalism and eventually to vindictiveness and to mindless destruction. Since the outbreak of hostilities, ironically, it had become more peaceful in the East End than for some years. Eric had been reluctant to close his school but he had eventually affiliated with the Labour League of Youth and had continued with meetings at his own house. Dot was still Eric's lieutenant and mainstay and broadened the diet of politics and international affairs by continuing her readings from the classics and by taking the members whenever possible to any dramatic performances, rare though they were becoming.

When Beccy had given a full account of herself Dot wondered whether she would consider helping her at the school. Dot's qualifications lay in Domestic Science but she had been forced to take on a more general role. Thirty-eight children had arrived for schooling, despite the authority's plea to parents not to allow their children to return to the city, and the numbers grew almost daily. An acting head-teacher had been appointed; an elderly man who had been through the last war, or the 'last one' as he called it. He and Dot had prepared something approaching a time-table to cover the children's needs, whose ages ranged from nine to fifteen.

"Would you consider joining us; unqualified, untrained and unpaid?" asked Dot.

Then they had a good laugh despite the desperate seriousness of the situation. Dot was dedicated to the aim of purposeful education, knew Beccy's character (which she had been partly instrumental in forming,) hoped she would give the matter some consideration, but had no intention of bringing pressure to bear. They parted with a hug and Beccy promised to see Dot again one evening of the following week.

Chapter Twenty-Eight

When Beccy arrived home it was Tom she saw first. He was engaged in building wooden railings at the front of the house to support the poor smokey-London privet hedge. The original railing, a rather grand filigree iron structure, had been commandeered, cut off with oxy-acetylene gas and collected by the local authority to provide iron for armaments.

Indoors, Leo was engaged in dispatching an order of 'battle-dress' blouses and Rachel was in the kitchen. The kitchen was now the operations centre of the house, large enough to hold a farmhouse table where the family and all the employees could meet and sometimes have refreshment. It was as well the kitchen was so commodious because the semi-basement parlour had been deemed a suitable shelter against air-raids. The Radstones had been provided with three cage-like structures made of angle iron, sheet metal and wire netting, and instructed to place them in the semi-basement close to the large chimney breast. Tom had erected them and carried downstairs single mattresses, one each for Rachel, Leo and Beccy. But they continued to sleep upstairs and were dreading the night, for they presumed it would be at night time, when they would have to shelter in their cages. They would not deter a direct hit, nothing would, they were told, but they should prevent smothering debris.

The evenings were beginning to lengthen and Beccy tried riding her old bicycle again. Tom had prepared it when he knew what she wanted it for and was pleased to see her pedal away to his parents' house. He had provided her with small lamps which were allowed only to glimmer in the blackout; and he called out that he would join her in about an hour.

Eric met Beccy outside the house door. He was wearing a tin-hat and was off to the fire-fighters' headquarters at the Citadel. He kissed Beccy, who smiled as she had to duck under the brim of his hat, as he walked away into the darkness.

Beccy had come as promised and wished to offer her services, for a trial period, if Dot thought she could be of use. The women were so attuned they were quickly able to reach decisions. Beccy would come to school in the morning which was scheduled to start at ten o'clock. And Dot explained the current position. Eight of the children were hoping to continue studying for the School Certificate. They had been studying a foreign language for between one and four years, so there would be a wide range of requirement. Four would want German, three French and one Spanish. Dot had been taking a boy at her house in the evenings through a course of Spanish and was prepared to continue.

"If you would take the German and French that would be an enormous help," said Dot. "I have not managed to get the Oxford syllabus, but it has been promised."

Beccy thought about the proposition and agreed to report to the school on the following day. She did. Three huge classrooms had been adapted. The head-teacher had fifteen children in his class, Dot had the same number and Beccy was introduced to the eight studying foreign languages. The boy doing Spanish joined them, as he was generally interested. Although in a dilapidated condition, the text books were in plentiful supply, because not much apparatus had accompanied the evacuees. Writing paper was at a premium but the problem had been partially overcome by the expedient of improvising on the reverse side of smooth wall-paper; the rolls had been cut into foolscap-size sheets. Beccy correctly guessed who had prepared the paper and confirmed it with Tom that evening.

The children rattled around in the barn-like rooms. They were eager to learn and were very pleased to be in a place which they trusted to be secure. Nearly all the parents had paid work now and were pleased to leave their children in good hands. Dot and Beccy made a simple lunch and within a few days were accompanied by half a dozen of the smaller children. Their numbers grew daily and it had eventually to be agreed that 'teacher' would provide only a warm drink and that the children should bring sandwiches if they wished to remain on the premises at midday. It was then that the head-teacher went over to the Marquis of Granby "for a bite," as he put it.

Beccy made quick progress and enjoyed the company of the children which was reciprocated. Dot was thrilled the older ones were having such good tuition in languages, and the head was pleased because he had fewer children to teach himself. He seemed to make up the rules as time progressed and decided to finish the term's teaching at the end of July. The Local Authority, seeing the school as a social success, if not necessarily educationally, would have preferred to remain open in August but had to concede everyone needed a holiday. The first Monday in September was the agreed date for reopening.

Chapter Twenty-Nine

I t was now generally agreed that the 'Phoney War' had come to an end. The education authorities implored the parents not to retrieve their children from their evacuation, and largely this request had been honoured. But the school had now almost doubled in numbers and a new teacher was added to the staff. And while the skies overhead raged the people of London were becoming acclimatised to the new demands being made on their lives.

The dock-lands of East London were being increasingly savaged by bombing raids. The enemy was dropping incendiary devices, interspersed with high explosive. Dornier and Heinkel aeroplanes pounded the area night after night. On one occasion Beccy had arrived home after school and was helping Rachel prepare the evening meal. They heard the air-raid siren wail followed closely by distant thuds. These sounds were becoming sufficiently familiar to cause no panic. People had even become used to gauging distances, direction and possible location of a raid. The evidence this evening spelt quite clearly East End. Although they were separated by only some four miles from the devastation they felt comparatively isolated from the event, such was the mixture of familiarity and fear that conditioned their emotion.

But personal tragedy struck. During the course of the raid, at about midnight, Dot's house had been caught in the midst of saturation bombing. Eric, on fire-watch duty, was patrolling his own street. The incendiaries screamed down and with horror he saw his own house ablaze. He tripped and fell over hoses and raised paving stones to get nearer.

"No entry! No entry!" shouted a voice in the darkness, above the noise of crackling timber, falling masonry and the sickly sound of water cascading from walls and sizzling into the molten ashes. Afterwards, no one was prepared to say whether they thought Eric had heard the order. The fire-fighting teams complained they could hear nothing except the whistle-commands, and these were often misinterpreted.

Eric climbed over the pile of sodden rubble that had once been his house. He was shouting out, "Dot, Dot, Dot. Tom! where are you?"

As he grappled with the broken timbers a beam from an upper storey fell across his back and killed him instantly.

Members of his team could not get near to the site owing to the intense heat, and it was not until the early hours of the morning that they forced an entry through the few remaining timbers. Then, voices were heard. Whistles sounded out and work stopped elsewhere as the rescue crews concentrated on this one site. Gradually they were able to excavate Dot and Tom from the rubble.

Miraculously they had sustained only slight injuries. Tom was out of control, angry and irreconcilable. In the darkness, above the noise of the fire he had heard his father shouting out their names. Tom yelled and yelled. He could not escape from the room. The door was blocked by fallen masonry. And now, even as he was being pulled free from the wreckage he saw a stretcher being carried down the street. It bore the body of his father.

Dot received many letters and messages of condolence. Eric had been a popular man. He had been appreciated in his work place, respected as a neighbour and honoured in the Movement of the Left. But it was in sincere regard for Dot's fortitude and dignity that the sentiments were addressed.

From the wreckage, Dot had been able to gather together very few of her belongings. Most had been destroyed by fire or ruined by the hoses and the water. The small items that were saved were taken by hand to the Hampstead Road House. Beccy gave Dot her room and transferred to Joseph's room which was smaller. Tom refurbished a room on the top floor, and erected two more cages in the semi-basement.

It was from Hampstead Road that the cortege left. The hearse arrived from the Royal Free Hospital and the mourners followed as the driver chose his way carefully. There were many small diversions to be made owing to the bomb-damaged houses and the closed-off streets. Dot sat next to Beccy in the leading car. From the windows of the car, the graffiti on the walls was easily discernible. The fading ones were still indicating "KILL JEWS KILL REDS," "IRA" and "KEEP THE EMPIRE." The freshly daubed signs declared "JOE FOR KING" and most prolific of all, signs declaring "SECOND FRONT NOW."

A very simple graveside ceremony took place at Bunhill Fields on this dismal December afternoon. Rachel had asked those wishing to return, to join them at Hampstead Road. Very few did come back. The evening was drawing in, travelling was difficult and people did not like to be away for very long from their own homes. Robert Moser and Beccy looked after those who did attend. Dot appeared to be composed and affable in contrast to Tom who was devastated. He was unable to be sociable. The mourners made full allowance and were sensitive to his feelings.

Chapter Thirty

I t was near to midnight when the occupants at the Radstones' were awakened by a hammering on the front door. Undisturbed nights were becoming a rarity now, but no one had heard the air-raid siren or the thud of bombs falling. Aircraft had been heard but everyone was inured to that droning sound.

Leo opened the door to two Military Policemen demanding to know if Thomas Fisher lived here. By this time Tom had raced down the stairs.

"You Thomas Morley Fisher?"

Tom agreed he was. The police produced a warrant for his arrest and told him to get a small bag of personal things together. They wanted to offer no explanation but upon pressure from Dot, the assembled, confused company were told that Thomas Morley Fisher had not responded to the order on his call-up paper. They tried to explain to the police that he had received no such demand; his house had been destroyed; perhaps the letter had been misdirected. It was all to no avail and when Tom was dressed he was pushed into the back of a van where two other men were sitting under escort.

"Knightsbridge Barracks," they shouted as they drove off into the darkness.

Robert was resident that night and he and Beccy decided immediately to go to the police station in Bow Street. They clung to each other in the pitch darkness. They had to stop several times. The pavements were uneven and it was difficult crossing roads owing to temporary barriers. There was no vehicular traffic about and the only people they saw were Local Defence Volunteers, guarding premises and A.R.P. wardens who shouted out when they heard their footsteps.

At Bow Street they were surprised to see a queue of people. A sergeant and a constable were patiently trying to resolve problems ranging from lost animals, to providing bedding for people who had suddenly been made homeless. After an hour of waiting and hearing all the queries and responses they arrived at the counter. The constable did not know how to deal with their problem and handed them over to the sergeant's queue. And it was another five minutes before they were attended to.

All the help they were given amounted to an acknowledgement that much of the post had gone badly astray during the past fortnight. It was highly probable that the mail had been kept in the *'poste restante'* department at Mount Pleasant; had they tried there?

Beccy and Robert traipsed all the way back to Coldbath Square and at three o'clock in the morning on a cold winter's day managed to retrieve the mail directed to Dot's address. They found one letter in a brown envelope bearing the royal coat of arms. It was directed to Mr. T. M. Fisher. They arrived back at Hampstead Road before light. Everyone was up and dressed. Dot wanted to set off for Knightsbridge immediately. Beccy wanted no refreshment and Robert insisted on taking them by car; petrol was rationed but the question was not even considered.

When they arrived at the barracks it was still dark. Tom was spending a miserable night in the cells. The orderly officer had him released immediately, once the position had been explained and the envelope stamped *'poste restante'* produced. They were all directed to the department of recruitment in the same building. New papers were issued to Tom for which he had to sign, ordering him to present himself at this place in seven days' time. Dot became angry and tried to extract at least an apology, for what she claimed amounted to false imprisonment. But no apology was forthcoming. The duty night-clerk looked sorrowful and tired but was unable to offer any shred of comfort.

"Let's get home," Tom said.

They all trouped out, exhausted, and hardly spoke again until they were all seated in Rachel's warm kitchen.

Chapter Thirty-One

In January of 1941 Beccy received a letter from Bernadette. It was full of her news; how she was coping with her new position, and how she was trying to keep one eye on the antiques market in her little spare time. She asked after the family and particularly about Beccy's plans. She did not mention the one thing Beccy most hoped to hear. Did not even mention his name. In disbelief, she paused in her reading. When she had sufficiently collected herself she read on. There was a poste script. If she were still interested she should report to Squadron Leader R. H. Murray at his temporary headquarters in the buildings of Lord's Cricket Ground. She should telephone to make an appointment. The number was appended.

Beccy hardly knew what to make of Bernadette's cryptic message. She considered it for several days but resolved nothing. Then, almost on impulse she decided to make the telephone call which resulted in an appointment being made with Squadron Leader Murray.

Beccy arrived at Lord's Cricket Ground. Hundreds of people were milling around and the loudspeakers were broadcasting the Air Force March, double forte. Squadron Leader Murray met her in his office; pictures of, what she assumed to be, famous cricketers lined the oak panelled walls. They conversed in English, French and German which made the intercourse no more difficult for Murray than it did for Beccy. As time passed it was doubtful whether they could have told a third party at which precise moment any one of the languages was being used. The conversation consisted of not much more than generalities. Murray, it transpired, was an old friend of Bernadette's. He had known her husband well; they had been up at Cambridge together. He had not seen Bernadette for a few years and had been agreeably surprised to have her letter.

The letter must have contained quite a lot about me, thought Beccy, for he was asking very few questions. But he did want to know about her recent visits to Paris and Berlin, with precise dates and the names of the hotels where she had stayed. And finally, would she be interested in joining the WAAF? Then he repeated what Bernadette had told her a year ago: the pressing demand for skilled linguists both in the field of instruction and as interpreters. The need was urgent; could she make her decision and if she wanted to proceed let him know the following week?

On the journey home Beccy's mind was in turmoil. Prompted by Squadron Leader Murray's mention of 'instruction' her thoughts had flown to Dot. The school building had been damaged by enemy action and was now closed as being unsafe. No plans had been made to restart the children's education, but Beccy had arranged to continue privately coaching in German, one boy and one girl, as they were approaching Matriculation. The Old Bakery was one of the few buildings to remain undamaged in the street and Chas and Maddy had readily agreed that Beccy should meet her two students there on two evenings a week. The students lived nearby and the engagement was kept on the strict understanding that if the air-raid siren should sound, they would not leave their homes. Quite good progress was made with their studies and though far from confident, Beccy and the students felt they were giving the subject their best effort. Only a few days before the school had been bombed, the local authority had, in response to Dot's continued appeals, agreed to pay Beccy as an unqualified teacher at the rate of twenty-four pounds a month. Beccy had her two students very much in mind. Perhaps she would be able to help them with their studies before the WAAF's "urgent need of her services."

At home that evening Uncle Ruben came to supper. The four of them enjoyed each other's company. Rachel was a good cook, but rationing prevented her from providing as she would have preferred. The chief ingredients of the meal were potatoes and conversation.

Beccy always discussed openly with her family, and her encounter at Lord's provided the main course. Leo thought an instructor's job would at least be safe, but he kept his counsel. Rachel could not understand how any woman would want to join the armed forces but she knew Beccy would, in any case, arrive at her own decision. Uncle Ruben wanted to know which cricketers' photographs were displayed at Lords.

But after supper, when they were alone, he said to Beccy, "Of course you know it will kill your father if anything happens to you."

The next morning Squadron Leader Murray's secretary was able to confirm a meeting with Beccy at Lord's for the day after tomorrow. Beccy was surprised the arrangement had been made so easily and the speed of events added a little piquancy to her routine. Then she recalled Murray's sense of urgency. The day after tomorrow could not come quickly enough.

This meeting at Lord's proved to be of a much more formal nature than her first encounter. She found herself facing a selection-committee of four. Murray was in the chair, another Squadron Leader sat at his right hand and two women, one in uniform, sat at his left. She was not introduced but Murray did stand to greet her. The committee knew a great deal about her, about her parents, her brother's work at De Havilland's, about her close friends whom they named, and about the recent acceptance as an unqualified teacher. After about half-an-hour's interview she was asked to wait in the ante-room. There she was offered a cup of tea by an orderly who called her "Miss." She accepted and was given a mug of tea which had been sweetened with condensed milk. She sipped it and hoped the orderly had not seen her grimace.

She was called back into the interview room. Murray was alone, and to her surprise all he said was,

"If you are still interested in joining the Forces report to the recruiting office tomorrow morning. You'll find it in the compound. Good day Miss Radstone, thank you for your time."

Beccy felt quite deflated and was glad to get back home, have some refreshment and hurry away to Chas and Maddy's to coach her two sensible students.

Chapter Thirty-Two

That night Beccy told her parents she had decided to enlist in the WAAF. To that end she duly set out for Lord's the following morning. Although still fairly early in the day, the place was throbbing with life. Men in civilian clothes and some looking awkward in new uniforms seemed to be moving everywhere. And the Air Force March still blazed through the speakers. After making enquiries, she was told that Lord's Grounds had no recruiting office for WAAF and the nearest was in Albany Street. She was perplexed and wondered how Murray, a senior officer in the R.A.F., could make such an elementary error.

It was a fine morning and she decided to walk through Regent's Park. She sat on her favourite bench watching the ducks. She had sat here in the past and had conversations with her mother and with Bernadette. There was time for contemplation. She had no immediate employment; her temporary unqualified status with the education authority had been withdrawn almost before it had begun! She would have been welcomed into the firm by Robert and her father to help with their swelling order book; she assumed there was employment in engineering. Joe had said they needed hands, especially women at his aircraft factory. And at the back of her mind she still hoped to be able to help her two language students for another few weeks. The morning was not turning out to be anything she had imagined. She retraced her footsteps and slowly walked back to Hampstead Road.

Tom was no longer present and although the place hummed with activity everyone felt his absence. Dot was still in mourning and considerably subdued. She was more than a guest and like Tom was included as family. She had two pressing problems and wished to involve Beccy in their resolution. The first was a legal matter concerning either compensation for her house, which was now totally demolished; or the acceptance of suitable accommodation in lieu. The second was her concern about the schoolchildren who had now taken to roaming the streets. She had persuaded the local authority that a crypt at the Old Citadel would make fair temporary premises. She had already enlisted some of the children's mothers to help tidy the room and the Salvation Army provided assistance with rudimentary decoration and furniture. Some tables and desks, chairs, books and other light apparatus was moved from the old school.

In the event, very few children attended The Citadel. There was a pervading fear of assembly without adequate (and official) air-raid protection. The education afforded was of the most basic kind and generally Dot found herself looking after about a dozen children of eight and nine years old, without official sanction. None of the older children came and the infants were mostly kept at home or looked after by Gran. To make a start, the parents agreed with Dot they would meet once a week on a Monday morning. Dot tried to plan individual assignments for the children. She would then check their homework, hear them read, do a few sums and some handwriting, and set the work for the following week. It was all makeshift and inadequate and Dot was far from satisfied. This was the project in which she hoped to involve Beccy. And Beccy agreed to accompany Dot to the Citadel to experience the problem. But unfortunately, after attending on only three occasions she felt herself to be out of her depth with the needs of the small children, and asked to be excused the task. Dot had reluctantly to agree.

Beccy continued working with her two older students who were now close to sitting their examination. She also helped in her father's workshop, but without much personal satisfaction. The sewing machines throbbed all day now and sometimes continued into the night. The staff had been increased and Rachel and Beccy found the home effectively reduced in size, confining them to the semi-basement area of the house. So, in March 1941, with a feeling of some dissatis-faction and unfulfillment, she made her way to the recruiting office.

Chapter Thirty-Three

It was a small office in part of a large barrack-like building on Albany Street. The door had glass panels and the sticky tape covering the panes partly obscured the view. She could see inside; one woman in an officer's uniform was sitting at a table. Beccy knocked and entered, was greeted with a smile and then for once in her life was tongue-tied.

At last she said; "I attended an interview with Squadron Leader Murray three weeks ago." The officer looked faintly puzzled but did not interrupt Beccy who was adding lamely "He told me if I were interested in joining the WAAF I should report to the recruitment centre at Lord's."

"No, we have no recruitment office there," said the officer, "the RAF has."

Beccy wondered why she was feeling slightly hostile. She could not in fairness, blame the woman before her now but she nevertheless asked rather tartly; "What relevance is there between the interview I underwent with Squadron Leader Murray and my presence here now". She felt foolish and out of character as she spoke.

Beccy was asked to take a chair. The woman seemed quite motherly. She did not know the Squadron Leader Beccy had named; had never heard of him. She had not before had a potential recruit, if that was what Beccy was, claiming to have been previously interviewed.

"Do you want to join up?"

The procedures were explained. A fairly simple form had to be completed which, in addition to personal details asked for special interests, hobbies and experiences of foreign travel.

"But I have already completed a similar form for Squadron Leader Murray." This remark was met with a quizzical if sympathetic look.

"Would you like to take the form home and think it over?"

Beccy stood and looked around the office. It was drab. One beam of sunlight shone from a high window encasing a shaft of lazy dust particles. The brown paint of the dado was peeling and the spare wooden furniture looked as though it had been removed from a bombed-out house. The contrast between this place and the razmataz at Lord's was palpable. No wonder Murray had not mentioned Albany Street, or was he testing her, she thought. And the thought crossed her mind that this was probably a sample of the worth placed upon women recruits by the authorities in contrast to the men. She sighed. A decision had to be made. Either she worked with her father or she would be directed into some other employment. Her temporary teacher status offered no immunity.

She picked up the proffered form and signed it. Then she recalled she had been asked to sign no forms after her interview at Lord's. The woman officer thanked her, called her "dear" and said she would be hearing from Headquarters soon.

"How soon?" asked Beccy.

"Probably within fourteen days."

Beccy walked back to Hampstead Road. Well, she had done it! She and Rachel had lunch together in the kitchen. Beccy felt strangely depressed. What had she achieved? Where was she going? Although she was in a mood of self-doubt she retained the presence of mind to conclude that many people felt similarly 'at sea' these days. She dragged herself away from introspection to see how she could help in the workshop.

The call-up paper arrived sooner than expected. With the letter came a travel warrant to be used to get her a medical examination in Edgware. The medical was straightforward and quite ordinary. She would be notified of the result within a week.

Back at home there was little to speak about at supper. Robert often stayed for an evening meal because work continued into the night on many occasions, but he was not present now, neither was Dot. Leo and Rachel stood with Beccy with hands gently touching around a lighted candle and remained quiet for a minute before the meal. They had not observed this ritual for many months and the quiet of the kitchen was therapeutic.

Chapter Thirty-Four

Beccy reported for duty, to the foyer of a large cinema at Swiss Cottage. It was her birthday; she was twenty-two. There were some twenty other women there, some obviously with their mothers. Some looked like schoolgirls, no older than Beccy's students. Some were talking loudly and excitedly but most of them stood as strangers, only gradually forming little knots of twos and threes. A uniformed woman with three stripes on her tunic had a clipboard, and was calling the women to gather round. Names were called. They were not all answered; it seemed they would give them thirty minutes. Meanwhile, if they would like a cup of tea "on the house" go and get it! A few of the younger recruits giggled and went to the cafeteria. The half-hour became an hour and the little group learned their first lesson in His Majesty's Service; something to do with waiting, hanging about.

The missing people did not arrive and the bus driver impatiently reminded the sergeant they ought to be on their way. She called out that everyone should go to the lavatory. Some did and eventually they were all ushered into the coach.

"Smokers at the back," shouted the sergeant, who joined the younger women on the rear seat.

Beccy sat next to a woman who appeared to be of her own age. The coach trundled slowly away from London on the Great North Road, and swung to the west at Barnet. Unless you were familiar with

98

the countryside it was difficult to tell where you were. All the sign-boards had been removed. Even shop names that might have presented a geographical clue had been obliterated. Some of the girls called out where they were and seemed to know everything. They managed to hold several conversations at once and to command attention over the length of the bus. They embarrassed the driver by first asking his name and then coaxing him for the destination. They got nothing from him except a request to go back and sit down. They got more from the sergeant who said they would be travelling about thirty-five miles. It was not until that evening they found they had arrived in Leighton Buzzard.

On arrival the sergeant tried to smarten her group of recruits. They were indeed a motley crew; not to mention some of the inappropriate footwear. And their hand luggage did not help to sharpen the image. The sergeant got them into a Nissen hut as quickly as possible. There were twelve iron beds in each hut; they had been allocated two Nissens. The youngsters ran out together to the "other one," leaving behind the more staid women who took a bed space each on which they dumped their luggage. Some people had far exceeded the clothing requirements and were ordered to post home the excess baggage.

It was a restless night in the Nissen hut. Beccy and a few of the quieter women had gravitated to the far end, leaving the more extrovert recruits nearer to the door. The girls from the adjacent hut kept popping back; there seemed to be constant trafficking. In the morning when Beccy went to the ablutions-hut she passed all the beds bearing sleeping occupants. Even the corporal's "Wakey-wakey" had failed to rouse some, who had to be prodded to consciousness.

First parade after breakfast was for "kitting out." Another Nissen hut! A kitbag! A slowly moving queue! Items of various shapes were tossed into each bag by staff on the other side of the counter, who were supposed to nominate each piece of equipment, though few did. Then the "flight," as they were now called, were hastened back to their quarters. It was as though the sergeant could not yet risk them to public exposure. She ordered all her contingent into one hut and told them to gather round. Then like a professional conjurer she produced items singly from her sample kitbag, expounding on each. First was a button-cleaning device.

"In the WAAF every item is either clean or filthy. No in-betweens. My flights are always clean and I win all the prizes," she added menacingly. No item was too small for her comment.

"This is a house-wife." She held up for inspection a wallet of soft linen. "A hussive," she added as an introduction to the argot. "Containing needle, fine, one; needle, crewel, one; thimble, one; suspender, clip-on, one; elastic white, one yard ....," she itemised, not omitting cottons, coloured. Beccy thought it would have been impossible to explain "kitting out" to a stranger, but for her group the whole procedure was proving to be hilarious. The sergeant had a word for every single item of clothing, keeping her pièce de résistance until last. She held aloft a pair of blue-grey bloomers.

"Knickers," she intoned and waited for silence. She had honed her next remark on the last six intakes. "Women's Auxiliary Air Force, personnel, for the use of." Again she paused, then; "Wear them! When you fall over I only want to see one colour."

Training at this induction unit included lectures on Administration, which meant the interpretation of orders as it affected members of the Services; King's Regulations. Beccy found the hilarity of the younger members quite surprising, particularly as they were now subject to two sets of laws, military and civil. The lectures were punctuated with drill, parade-ground drill and physical training (which amounted to drill.) They had to be trained for cross-country runs of two miles and six-mile route marches with back-packs. But most of the time was spent either in the kitchens, preparing vegetables, in the hut cleaning shoes and buttons or washing and ironing clothes. Despite the fatigues, the six week course, which sheltered under the title "basic training," passed quickly. At the end of this period, the women, apart from a couple who had been withdrawn, had metamorphosed into a semblance of a unit which could respond fairly reliably to military-style commands. They even had a passing out parade.

Some of the women were promoted to the rank of "Aircraft Woman First Class," which seemed to have been reserved for those going on to "signals." Beccy was not one of those and when shown their official report noted that the column headed "trade" was completed with the legend "General Duties." The majority of the women were then posted to a unit as near to their homes as possible.

Chapter Thirty-Five

Beccy found herself with three others at a barracks in Albert Road. Originally designated luxury flats the buildings had been purchased by the War Office and converted. The women were allocated a room for four and they settled in like seasoned troopers. They were unprepared for the next turn of events, however.

Their "General Duties" translated into skivvying and cooking in the many canteens that surrounded Regent's Park. There were thousands of men billeted in converted flats similar to their own. The great majority of them were in transit. They possessed enormous appetites and were fed three meals a day. All the dirtiest jobs went to the new intake and Beccy found herself in the sculleries scouring the pots for eight hours a day.

After one week she was given a twenty-four-hours pass. She walked through the park automatically saluting the officers she passed. She had been absent for only six weeks yet she looked at Hampstead Road with new eyes. As she approached her house she purposely looked up to see if the slogan was still visible from the street. It was. From the top of the front steps she mouthed: "AS YE RIP SO SHALL WE SEW."

Through the window she spotted her father. Her beloved Dad. He looked thin and poor and wore small silver-framed spectacles over myopic eyes. Here was the great heart of her family who, with his wife, had struggled his way through poverty and privation years ago, from a country with whom they were now at war. Total war. He did not look up but continued closely to inspect the garment in his hand. It apparently achieved his seal of approval. He placed it in the cardboard dispatch-box and then saw Beccy through the window. She smiled and kissed the pane of glass. He hastened to open the door and they rushed down to the kitchen to find Rachel.

Beccy was very pleased to have her father's hands make subtle alterations to her uniform. He sniffed at the material and looked closely at the weaving and the stitching. He said little. Rachel looked at Beccy's hands and was alarmed at their rough state, and broken finger nails. She set about manicuring and fussing. It was unlike Rachel to fuss but Beccy quite enjoyed the attention. It was not long before the inevitable thought was aired.

"Is this what Bernadette had in mind for you? It couldn't be. There has been a mistake. Have you written to her?"

Beccy had written to her, from Leighton Buzzard, but had not received a reply.

The twenty-four hours flew and Rachel walked once again with Beccy across the park. They stopped for just a few minutes on their favourite bench, then parted, both turning after a hundred yards to wave.

Back at the barracks work continued grindingly. Beccy learned that she would be allowed a twenty-four-hour pass each week which would normally give her Mondays free. She arranged, by letter to meet her two students on Mondays. Chas and Maddy continued to make their room available. At first they met at six o'clock but they all agreed afternoons would suit them better. This arrangement held for a few weeks and the students put special effort into their programme of revision. These occasions became the slender threads that kept her sanity.

She returned to her billet to continue polishing her shoes, polishing her buttons and peeling potatoes. Hundredweights of them. Sometimes they were joined in the task by a few young men who, for some minor misdemeanour, had been sent to peel potatoes as a punishment. They managed to sit around a bucket talking and joking all the time. When one man threw his potato into the bucket they all threw one, peeled or not.

Beccy received further promotion later that day. At lunch time when the men queued at the serving hatch she wielded a three-inch brush which she had dipped into a vat of molten margarine. The men held a piece of bread on the palm of the hand and Beccy wiped the brush on to the bread so proffered. Fortunately the constantly moving line of men allowed little time for banter.

For several days running Beccy noticed a blond haired boy, who looked about fourteen, sitting at the potato bucket. She asked him what on earth he had been up to. She was taken aback by his reply. He had really done nothing amiss but joined the working party just to come and see her. He had started at Art school, got his course deferred, joined the RAF as aircrew in training and spent the last three weeks marching around Regent's Park. Would Beccy meet him outside? They could talk about art and perhaps visit a gallery. Beccy explained to the boy that she had only Monday mornings free.

He persisted. "Could I see you next Monday?"

"How do you know you will be free on Monday morning?" she asked.

"Please," he said. "I will meet you outside the entrance to your block at ten."

Beccy thought he would not be there and wondered what on earth she was doing. Then she wondered how he knew where her living quarters were.

They did meet, however, and walked toward Trafalgar Square. She had not discussed art or paintings since her busy days with Bernadette and it was pleasant relief to be away from the kitchens. He looked even more of a boy now as he walked beside Beccy in his new uniform and creaking boots. Very few paintings were being exhibited at the National Gallery. Only three rooms on the ground floor held an exhibition at the present time, and they were all of contemporary works. The old masters were stored away in the country for safety, they were told. As they came out into the sunlight they read a poster advertising lunch-time concerts at St. Martin-in-the-Fields. They crossed the road. Today Campoli was playing the Mendelssohn Concerto. The concert was free and the Church was packed. Most of the audience was in uniform of one kind or another. The performance was rivetting. The boy reached for Beccy's hand in excitement. She felt strangely maternal, as though she were taking her son to his first concert. They had a snack in the crypt and Beccy said she would have to hurry home.

"Where is home?" he wanted to know.

Beccy did not want to encourage him. They walked into Charing Cross Road and he saw her on to a twenty-nine bus.

"Thank you," he said. "See you tomorrow, thank you."

Chapter Thirty-Six

When Beccy arrived at Hampstead Road two letters awaited her; one from Bernadette and one from Tom. He was training in North Yorkshire, missed home terribly, had no news, sent love to all and kisses for her and would she write? Bernadette's letter too was affectionate and simple. She had been in America for eight weeks on some kind of course which she did not specify, had now returned home and was due in Belfast for a week in April. Could Beccy come to see her?

Beccy did not even have time to change out of her uniform before hurrying off on her bicycle to the East End and her two students. They were surprised! They had not seen her so garbed before. They told her they thought the uniform made her look younger. They worked conscientiously then until nearly seven when they dispersed.

At Hampstead Road Dot joined the little family for supper and was glad to see Tom had written. He had not corresponded with his mother for some weeks. Robert was there and so was Joe who had cycled all the way down from Hatfield. The evening passed too quickly. Joe and Robert accompanied Beccy back to her billet. She signed in at 23.45, the latest she had ever recorded. Some of the younger women ribbed her as a "stop out" as she climbed the stairs to her room. All three of her companions were in bed, probably asleep.

The following morning the usual small crowd was gathered around the notice board. Everyone was supposed to read Daily Routine

Orders. A few did and passed on the information. Some passed the messages in a sense of friendship but one or two managed the pronged-barb of "knowing it first" and "you're for the high-jump" attitude. It was from one of the latter type that Beccy learned she was to report to the Adjutant's office at 09.30. So, direct from peeling onions, she reported to the Corporal Cook, and with some trepidation smartened herself for the Admin. Office.

The Adjutant came straight to the point. She was being posted. In service parlance her work here had been satisfactory and she was accorded 'average' grading. There was no other information. She could collect her rail pass and subsistence allowance of one shilling at noon from this office.

Beccy was beset with a confusion of mixed feelings and rushed to the kitchen where her room-mates were working, then up the stairs again to pack her kit. The corporal said she had rarely heard of such short notice being given but that was the Services for you.

At midday a driver took her to Marylebone Station and she caught the train to Berkhamsted. The train arrived on time and she was immediately met by a woman driving a camouflaged car. The driver wanted to be friendly but could not answer any of Beccy's questions. In what seemed to be a very short time they arrived at a large country house which was said to be near to Little Gadsden. Beccy walked as smartly as she could manage with a kit bag on her shoulder to the front door which was open. She peeped inside. After the daylight the contrast was too great to see very far. She dropped her bag and noticed it fell onto polished parquet flooring. And her first thought was that she would soon be on her knees polishing it. Hardly a reverie; she was surprised by the greeting of a woman in civilian clothes whom she thought seemed vaguely familiar.

"Welcome," she said. "Come into the kitchen."

Beccy thought that sounded about the right note. She was offered a chair and with pleasant informality they began to talk. It was almost like real conversation, but Beccy was not to be so easily disarmed. Then she was shown to a room which was to be hers. She could not believe her senses. The room was small but had a bed, a wardrobe, a chest of drawers, a table with a reading lamp, a wooden chair and a fireside chair. And there were also open bookshelves crammed with literature, from which she could barely refrain diving into immediately.   There was also a wash-hand basin, hangers in the cupboard and a full-length looking glass.

She was about to pinch herself when her escort said "Sorry there's no heating in here.   None of us has any.   If you are cold come down to the sitting room."

Beccy pinched herself.   But there were more surprises.   The dinner gong sounded at half past seven and Beccy was introduced to some of the 'guests;' no other word seemed appropriate.   The long refectory table of polished oak was simply and elegantly laid; linen napkins and glasses glinted and gleamed.   Then she became only too startlingly aware that hers was the only uniform to be seen around the table. When the orderlies appeared to serve the meal they too wore uniform. Beccy was convinced she was about to be humiliated and fairly publicly at that.   Despite the kindness of the men sitting on either side she felt prickly and unable to enjoy the food.   When the dinner was over she rose and the men beside her rose.   To cover her embarrassment she sought out the women who had met her; was it only two hours ago?

Her name was Danielle, everyone called her Danny.   Would Beccy please call her Danny?   Would she mind coming to the kitchen again? Beccy was less puzzled by the word this time and realised it was the hub of whatever activities they got up to.   Danny said that the course (unspecified) was to start in four days' time and that no leave would be available under any circumstances.   And just as Beccy thought she was getting used to the quirks, Danielle advised her she must take a seventy-two hours pass immediately.

"When you return wear civilian clothes.   Leave the uniform at home.   There is a train for town at ten twenty.   A driver will take you to the station."

Beccy moved off to get her things together, but there was a rejoinder.   Beccy was quickly to learn the importance to be attached to Danielle's parting words.

"Everything here is top secret.   Do not say anything about us to anyone; parents, friends, sweethearts; especially sweethearts.   See you on Saturday," she said with a beaming smile.

It was all too much to take in.   Beccy wondered what secret she was privy to.   It was not until she found herself on the cold, draughty platform at Berkhamsted that she believed her feet touched the ground.

Chapter Thirty-Seven

There was glad surprise when her mother opened the door. It was half past one in the morning. Straight to the kitchen, the range was still hot and Beccy suddenly recovered her appetite. That was a joyous night. Rachel, Leo and Beccy talked and listened, mostly talked, about everything, but Beccy kept Danielle's parting remark foremost in mind. She told them she had been posted to Little Gadsden, that was all. If her parents inferred anything from that they did not probe, especially when they knew she was to leave her uniform at home. They were all finally exhausted as the first rays of sunlight strayed through the high window.

This short leave was one of the happiest occasions they could remember. Rachel and Beccy spent nearly all the time together. Dot had decided to take up the offer of a flat in Finchley Road and was away making final arrangements, and Joe was back in Hertfordshire. Robert persuaded Leo to have a day off work. He did not know what a holiday was. He never took a day off. The two women almost frog-marched him out of the house. They took a bus to the embankment, walked west toward Chelsea and window- shopped. Poor Leo! The shops had not much to display. The frocks looked cheap but their price labels indicated differently and included the number of coupons required for purchase. The women had no intention of making a purchase, they were just thoroughly enjoying themselves. They had lunch, not the best food ever produced; and then wandered back to

South Kensington and found a train for Euston Square Station. The women were brimming with the satisfaction of having had a good day. Leo could hardly walk. He had never been a walker and as soon as he got home he put his feet into a bowl of hot soapy water and declared he would never go shopping with them again. They all creased with laughter including Robert who had come down to the kitchen to join in the merriment.

The short respite at home was recuperative but too fleeting. Beccy dressed in very sober clothes and carrying a small suitcase prepared to make her way back to Little Gadsden.

Chapter Thirty-Eight

She found Danielle as soon as she had hung her clothes in the cupboard and placed a few of her books on the shelves. Whether it was owing to Danielle's warm welcome or whether her own attitude had changed she did not know, but she became aware of a strong feeling of camaraderie. She had not experienced this sensation since her youthful days with Dot and Eric. She had always felt secure with family and close friends but never before with comparative strangers. And this sense of bonding became stronger with time.

"I'm Danny and everyone here is known by a first name only. You are Madeleine," she said with a laugh. Danny expounded at length: "Madeleine Ribierre is twenty-two years old. She was born soon after the marriage of Marcel and Beatrix Ribierre in 1920." The exact birth date was given along with her full address which they had occupied in Ribeauville. Danny continued, "Her father was a miner in the Ruhr; he was killed in a pit accident when she was eight. Beatrix Adeline struggled to raise her child, Madeleine Edna, and was pleased to pack her off to her brother who has a successful baker's shop-cum-cafe in St. Bernard, a small village near to St. Omer."

This information was all too much and she asked Danny to stop.

"It's OK," she said. "It's all written down for you. You must learn it. After all you are Madeleine. Now may I accompany you to your room?"

Danny brought a suitcase, opened it and asked Madeleine to sort through. It was full of clean but old clothing. All the items bore faded labels showing French manufacture.

"Choose your outfit," said Danny. "I'm afraid I have to stay while you dress." She took the discarded clothes, placed them in a bag and noted every item Beccy chose to wear, from the skin up. "You won't be getting these back for some time," Danny said, indicating the bag. "See you in the ante room about seven," and as she got to the door she said "Make an appointment with the hairdresser tomorrow," and as a parting shot, "Don't shave your armpits."

As the door closed Beccy looked into the mirror. She had already shortened her hair to collar-length and wondered what bobbed styling would feel like.

Chapter Thirty-Nine

On the following afternoon she found herself closeted with Frances. "It's a simple code name," said Frances.

Madeleine was to study maps and orienteering with her, especially detailing an area surrounding St. Omer. Every road of every village had to be learned, with the probable routes from St. Omer Railway Station to any given address. She had to learn local shop names, bus and tram routes with numbers. It all sounded formidable enough. But Frances knew her subject inside out and had spared no effort to make the task as interesting as possible. Maps of various scales were studied, right down to what Frances called 'Postmen's Maps' where every building and outhouse was represented. There were photographs of all kinds to be committed to memory, ranging from snap shots of families at picnic, standing outside their houses or proudly posing by newly acquired motor cars. There were aerial photographs showing roads, bridges, canals, railway lines, gas works and factories.

"Well, you've got to learn it all," said Frances. "Here, have a cigarette."

Madeleine said she did not smoke. Frances pushed a Gauloise into her mouth.

"Now light up," she said. "No, not from a match. Ask me for a light."

They joined cigarettes; Madeleine sucked and spluttered.

"Well, if you don't want to smoke it just let the smell permeate your hair and clothes."

Madeleine was feeling rather self-conscious about her hair. That morning she had been shorn. Quite a nice shape, but so out of character. That night Beccy looked at Madeleine in the glass. Perhaps it was not out of character. She pushed a beret on to her head and practised swearing at the image.

Next day she had special language lessons. She learned colloquialisms, dialect from the Ruhr, the latest jokes doing the rounds in St. Omer and the news of the war from the German propaganda machine. When she briefly returned to her room at break-time she discovered her few personal books had been removed together with her toiletries. Nothing of her own originality remained. At lunch time Danny apologised for going to her room.

In the afternoon it was maps, photographs and names again. Frances showed immense patience with her. As they sat together studying the material they could have passed for French sisters. Perhaps Frances was French, she seemed to favour that tongue. After an hour Madeleine thought she would explode, so they borrowed some running shoes and trotted around the ground for half an hour. They returned the shoes, had a shower and arrived in the ante room at seven.

"Have a drink," said Frances.

Madeleine knew it was an order, not a request.

"I'll try some sherry," she said.

Frances ordered two beers.

"But," began Madeleine.

"Just have a sip then and put a dab behind your ears." Every one around the bar laughed and they all dabbed beer behind their ears.

Most of the hubbub of conversation seemed to be French, but one man who was trying to explain an operational strategy, found it more readily expressible in German. Madeleine's ear was well attuned to the language and she fully realised that she was now an agent of Special Operations.

Chapter Forty

She was a conscientious student and gave every facet of the training her full endeavour. Gadsden House and grounds occupied some hundred acres of mixed woodlands. She was to explore this area in great detail during the next few weeks, but apart from the entrance gate she never found any other fenced boundary.

A French commando named Pierre had been allocated the task of instructing her in field exercises. Despite her being classified as non-combatant he insisted she should understand how to use a knife if only for self-defence. Madeleine was intrigued with his accent; from the north-west of France, she guessed. He confirmed this by telling her he had been brought up near Armentieres. And it was this intonation that she found herself absorbing.

Her field education included making a rough shelter and taking cover. Pierre showed her workable methods of survival, how to crawl while keeping the head down and on one memorable occasion, when it was teeming with rain, how to find water. That gave them a much needed opportunity for a breather and a laugh.

One day Pierre left her in a deep wood and told her to find her own way back. And suddenly, for the first time since her arrival at Gadsden she felt alone. The woodland was almost impenetrable; she certainly could not see where the sun should be, even had there not been low cloud. She tried to use her marching compass, but could get no sightings. So she scrambled about approximately working her way towards the south. She had a reliable wrist watch and found she had cleared the woodland in about half-an-hour. The trees had given way to downland and in the distance she saw a farmer ploughing with draft horses. It was a rare sight for anyone to come upon and intrigue took over from her exhaustion.

As she approached she called out "Hello! Can you tell me the way to Gadsden House?"

The man did not move his gaze from a distant point of reference. The beautiful shires and the man formed an harmonious team. At the end of the furrow he unhitched the plough, the horses wheeled, he recast the harness and came slowly back toward her. Without averting his eyes he drew up beside her and whoa'ed his team. He wiped his face and neck with a coloured cloth and then looked at her squarely.

"Lost are you?"

Madeleine readily admitted.

"You're not the first."

She wondered whether he was going to say any more. Then slowly he removed a bottle of cold tea from his coat pocket and swigged.

"Want a drink?" he offered.

"Why should a simple question like that present a problem?" she thought and said "Thank you."

He gave the neck of the bottle a twist with his fingers and offered it to her.

"How do I get to Gadsden?"

He smiled and pointed.

"Skirt the wood. Keep to the brow of the hill on the left. In about half a mile swing right on to a track by a barn. Got no roof," he chuckled. "Continue downhill for another half mile through a fire-break and you will come to a broad gravelled path leading to the House. Then you got another mile. What you doing there or shouldn't I ask?"

Madeleine thanked him and as the horses took up the strain, set off in the direction he had indicated. The sound of the horses' hooves plodding through the softened earth receded as she began her way back. Her eyes watered, whether from the wind which had risen or from the frustration of realising she had been completely lost in her own country not two miles from base, she wasn't sure. The farmer's directions were sound and she was glad to get her feet on the firm path back to Gadsden. Then she saw, in the distance, a figure walking towards her. It was of a well-made man, and good-looking too, she thought, as he came close.

"Good afternoon," he said, in French. "You're Madeleine."

It was Squadron Leader Murray; she had not seen him since her second interview at Lord's. His accent gave her a frisson of pleasure, her scalp tingled and she wondered he recognised her without her long hair. His conversation was urbane and contrasted strongly with Pierre's blunt commands. She was fairly exhausted owing to the day's exertions but rallied as he turned round and accompanied her to the House.

"I wanted to see how you were progressing. Danny says you are doing well."

"I have just managed to lose myself," she said simply.

"Pierre usually manages to leave his customers in the most impenetrable part of the wood. Did he do that?"

"I found a farmer and asked my way back."

"That's OK. Danny was at your interview, you know. She's picked a winner."

Madeleine could not have felt less like a winner at the moment. But it was cheering conversation and they separated at the house door. Unlike Danny, there was no parting shot from Murray but he had asked her if she had done any flying, and upon receiving a negative reply had said that would soon have to be remedied.

In her room she considered his last remark and then the man himself. Danny had said everyone here was known only by a first name. Murray's name was Edward. It suited him. But hardly anybody used it. Danny did. But she called him Eddy or more often "Eddy dear," but that was Danny! Although they all felt easy with him they were still inclined to say "Sir," quietly at the end of a sentence, to which he would incline his head slightly and raise his eyebrows as though mildly surprised. His mood rarely changed, but sometimes at Gadsden he would be less forthcoming and whisper went round that he had "Baker Street Blues." She learned that the hub of the Special Operations Executive was known as "The Baker Street Irregulars."

At dinner that night she sat next to Edward Murray. She looked around for Pierre but he was not present. She wondered mildly whether he had managed to find his way out of the woods.

116

Chapter Forty-One

Early the following morning she was driven to an airfield near to Coventry. She had been scheduled to have a flight in a Lysander aircraft for familiarisation. Arriving at about eleven o'clock she saw many young uniformed RAF men in groups, whom she learned were pilots under training. She expected to be taken to a briefing-office or to an operations room, but the car she was in was driven directly inside a hangar. There she was introduced to a mature-looking man dressed in soiled white dungarees.

"This is Madeleine," said the driver.

"My name's Arthur," he said, and as Madeleine registered the name he added with a smile: "Jim Arthur."

He explained that no Lysander was available, but he would give her a flight in a D.H. Tiger Moth. She wondered if Joe had helped to make the aeroplane. Then she startled herself as she realised Madeleine did not know any Joe at De Havilland's; and she dragged herself back to the job in hand. The little yellow biplane stood nearby and the pilot was talking to her. He gave her a flying-jacket, helped her into a parachute harness and a helmet and explained the inter-com as she struggled with the unfamiliar gear on the hangar's apron. He stood on the wing and helped her into the cockpit.

When she was securely strapped in, he fixed the speaking tube and climbed into the other cockpit. The engine was started by a mechanic who rotated the propeller and then disappeared under the wing to remove the chocks. They taxied out and stood at right-angles to the runway. Madeleine found the noise from the engine surprisingly dominant and could hardly hear what Jim was saying. He said little in fact; turned into the wind and seemed to speed across the field. She hardly knew when they left the ground behind and only became aware of being airborne when the climb was completed and the engine noise subsided. After a few minutes she heard a voice say that Coventry lay under their left wing and she should look down. The aeroplane banked steeply to the left and she clung desperately to the side of the cockpit. They straightened up and after what seemed an age he said that Leamington Spa was coming up and they would do another turn to port; she clung to the side. The voice told her to hold the joy-stick with her right hand and to put her feet on the pedals.

"Now put your hand on the throttle."

"What?" she managed to find her voice.

"That knob on the left. Put your hand on it."

She fumbled about and the voice through the tube told her to look at her left hand. She could not imagine why she had not thought of looking. Jim banked over Leamington and she felt the stick tilt and her feet move slightly. That turn did not hurt nearly so much. They levelled out and he said they were heading for Rugby.

"Look out for it!"

She looked out and began, if not actually to enjoy, at least to accommodate the experience. Jim told her to turn the aircraft left over Rugby.

"Good," he shouted. "Now head for home."

She found herself scanning the sky, then looking down for landmarks. Below she saw a railway line and with the sun on her left cheek followed it.

Jim landed and taxied to the hangar. He helped her out of the cockpit and grinned. They took off their flying helmets and she gave him the flying-coat.

"Good," he said. "Have you flown before?"

And only now he asks me, she thought.

"Many people are sick first time up," he said approvingly. "You are scheduled for another flight next week. I think we'll stick to the Tiger; do some navigation." He gave her an aerial map, taken from his office shelf, and asked her to study it.

Chapter Forty-Two

Over a period of time Frances had made a large collection of boxes: cereal boxes, cardboard tubes and any odd container she could find. With Madeleine she made a large model of the village of St. Bernard. A strip of toilet paper skewed diagonally across the floor of her room represented the main St. Omer Road. The boxes were used variously to represent the buildings which lined the roads. Her uncle's cafe and bakery stood proud in its original Shredded Wheat livery. The petrol station reduced to a Corn Flakes box and most of the village houses to match boxes. There were alleys, too, constructed from split-egg containers; and coloured paper marked the fields. Madeleine, in person, was represented by a pencil standing on a pierced eraser. Frances set her problems: when standing in this lane could she be observed from points A and B in the High Street? Which was the shorter route between A and B? Which might be safer in the dark and why? How could she get to and from the station: a. with the crowd, or b. alone?

Frances was a bit like Danny, she never let up. The only occasion when Madeleine saw her angry though was the time she was unable to answer quickly enough the names of the roads adjoining the railway station and the canal bridge to the north of St. Omer. She eventually arrived at the route but Frances was wild and stormed out of the room calling "It's your own life at stake."

Feeling very depressed Madeleine left the room herself and went outside into the fresh air. It was a beautiful afternoon. She had walked the grounds many times and now wanted to be out in a country lane. She arrived at the entrance and approached the gate. It was padlocked. A soldier materialised from a nearby hut.

"It's locked, madam."

Madeleine looked at him. "Well, open it please."

"Have you a pass, madam?"

She was irritated. She was not used to being "Madam'd." She had no pass. "I didn't know a pass was necessary," she said.

"Well it isn't in the grounds, Madam."

She gave up. And feeling less than mollified walked back to the house. In her room she tried desperately hard to practice some Morse Code.

A few days later she made the long, tedious journey to Coventry, but eventually felt rewarded by an exciting flight with Jim Arthur. In his small office inside the hangar they looked at the map he had given her. He was pleased she had absorbed so many details. They planned a three-legged cross-country flight; north to Loughborough then east to Cambridge where they would land at the University Air Squadron's field, have some lunch, then back to Coventry. He explained the rudiments of direct navigation and with the known wind speeds plotted vector diagrams. On a piece of card he recorded the compass directions they should follow and gave it to her. It was a thoroughly enjoyable experience undertaken on a beautifully calm day. All went well. Madeleine did some navigating, was intrigued with the refuelling procedure at Cambridge and felt she had something to write home about . Except that she could not. And that was a cause of some frustration, although back at Gadsden Danny's was a shoulder to lean on. Madeleine had never known a person quite like her. She mastered details, while managing to keep the main objective in sight. It was her war effort. She was a pillar of support to all the occupants and seemed to understand their frailties.

Madeleine retailed her day's flying to Danny. Danny said "Well done dear. I want you to be in the boiler room at six."

If anyone else had made that remark it would have been considered a laughable non sequitur. Not from Danny!

Madeleine found her way to the boiler room. Down a flight of wooden stairs from the main hall, on to a small landing and down a flight of stone steps. No one was there. The boiler had not been fired. It was gloomy, lit only by one small window, high up. Wood piles were stacked around the far wall, and near the door was a small table and chair. Madeleine's bewildered thought was interrupted as the door creaked open. A man entered. She could hardly see his face. He sat at the table.

"What is your name?" he fired, in immaculate German.

"Madeleine Ribierre." The answer came as a conditioned reflex.

"Why are you in St. Bernard?"

Then she knew it was all part of the drill and played her part accordingly. It droned on. Backwards and forwards. Question and answer. Question and answer. Stick to your simple brief. Do not deviate at all.

"What do you call your uncle?"

"Uncle," she said hesitatingly. First mistake! She knew what to expect.

"Uncle? Uncle who?"

She was grilled for about ten minutes. Then the man left as abruptly as he had come. To the best of her knowledge she had never seen him before. It had grown almost dark in the boiler room. From the wood pile there came a rustling sound. She looked across in time to see a rat stirring. She was not unduly alarmed. She had seen plenty of rats in the East End. What was she thinking? What East End? East End of Berlin? She had so much to learn.

She made her way slowly up the stone steps, then across the landing and up to the Hall. Danny was there. Of course Danny would be.

"Come and have a drink," she said.

"There are rats down there," said Madeleine.

"Mmmmm!" said Danny. "Two beers, please."

The following night, after dinner, the full moon shone and the terrace steps gleamed in reflection. A few of them decided to sit outside with their coffee. And then they saw it. They heard no sounds but on the southern horizon the sky over London began to glow; pink at first, then a deep red developing into a bright yellow half-globe of dazzling light. Somebody had heard the BBC evening news and relayed the message that large waves of bombers were at the eastern approaches and making their way up the Thames. The group of people on the terrace stood in awe, speechless and suddenly chill.

Madeleine sank on to a bench, her chin on her chest, scarcely breathing. She did not know for how long she stayed in that position. She was silent and motionless. Then an arm caressed her shoulder and she wept softly. It was not until they reached the dining room that she looked up to see the arm belong to Edward Murray.

"I will try to find out about your family," he said. Then after a long pause;

"Madeleine, I have really come to give you a message. Sorry to be so abrupt. The work you and Danny have been doing is proving successful and we now want something conveyed to your Uncle tomorrow night. It's a packet of information for him. You must not know of its contents. When you have landed, a reliable man will take it from you. We cannot be sure about the timing of the return-information so you will have to wait until your Uncle is ready to give it to you. Then we will get you back."

She had only a couple of hours fitful sleep and was poking about in her room when Danny entered. She was sorry to intrude, she said, but there were some last minute details to arrange, and she had to check Madeleine's dressing. She was as meticulous as ever, and made a note of all the garments worn. Madeleine, complete, wore a maroon home knitted jersey over a drab skirt. She had white ankle socks and stout but worn leather shoes which reeked of paraffin-wax polish. To top it off she wore a pinkish beret which covered all her hair. Her handbag, more like a satchel to be slung over one arm, had its contents tipped on to the bed and Danny tossed the items in as she recorded them. A comb; a cheap lipstick; a couple of grey-looking aspirin tablets which had rolled into the dusty crevices of the bag; a damaged carton containing a sanitary towel; some coins and a stub of pencil. Paper money, just a few francs in small denominations, was added and finally her identity card and a creased photograph of her father and mother taken on their wedding day.

The two women looked at each other. There was nothing left to say; but they hugged silently for a moment. Madeleine was driven to Cambridge and quickly transferred to a Lysander aeroplane which was flown south. As she looked out from the aircraft she could see dense clouds of smoke hanging over the estuary and obscuring London's docklands. She felt sick with apprehension and hoped and prayed her family and friends had been spared. She felt her powers of acting were being tested to the limit. She had been drilled into the "Madeleine" role and she had to force her thoughts to deal with the job in hand.

At midday they landed in Hawkinge and taxied into a hangar. She was escorted to a hut which served as a very primitive messing hall. She could not eat anything but was glad to have a glass of water. She was shown to a small room and advised to have a couple of hours' rest. She could not rest. The hut was oppressively hot, and she wandered out into the summer's afternoon. By teatime she had regained her composure and a small appetite. Although her briefing had been explicit, and despite her knowing only too well that "waiting was the name of the game", she was impatient.

She had been most disappointed that Jim Arthur had not piloted her from Cambridge, and was very relieved to see him later that evening. He was wearing uniform and she sensed he was in a much more serious mood than on previous occasions. She was handed a string-wrapped parcel and in the excitement of boarding the Lysander she could not think why the sisal-string under her fingers felt so evocative.

The moon was almost full and clear and hung low in the sky when they took off. The Kent coast was clearly defined and the ripples of the waves reflected the stray beams of moonlight. Surely the Germans must be aware of this flight; will have logged it on radar or something. At least the French aircraft spotters would have heard its engine as they crossed the coast. Jim was silent. His concentration was totally exclusive yet it was reassuring.

"We shall follow the river," he said eventually.

And as she looked down she saw a narrow ribbon of light, unmistakably Gravelines, and from memory she photographed the route to what she hoped would be a landing spot at Nieurlet.

"If no glim-lights are showing I shall turn round and go back."

They were flying fairly low, fifteen hundred feet and she said "Everybody will have heard us. We're sitting ducks, aren't we?"

She had asked the same question at Gadsden. The answer had been complicated. Very probably the enemy were well aware of these flights but there were priorities and a flight by a single Lysander did not amount to a hill of beans as the Americans were quick to remind everyone. They had taken all possible precautions, had made scrupulously detailed arrangements with the Resistance and had their fall-back plans. Jim did not mention, though, that he wore uniform in case of capture. His navigation was immaculate. He had found a glim-lighted path in a field and was preparing to land.

"As soon as I say 'Go!' jump out!" he said. "Touch down will be bumpy; run away from the aircraft as fast as you can. I shall be taxiing away immediately; you know the rest; good luck girl."

She did exactly what was expected of her. And she found her hand being held tightly as she was pulled across the field. At the bottom of a deep hedge she gave her parcel to Jacques.

"Just call me Jacques," he had said.

She heard the aircraft take off and saw several shadowy figures running to pick up the small glim-lights. Jacques must have passed her parcel immediately to a third party for she did not see it again. They were now trudging over fields, along little lanes, crossing canal bridges on the trek to St. Bernard. Apart from telling her his name Jacques said nothing on the walk. Taciturn for a Frenchman, she thought. Then as they approached the village he broke the silence.

"There's the bake-house. I shall enter and sit at a table. Give me a couple of minutes. You know what to do."

As Jacques entered the cafe she heard the door-bell clang from the other side of the road and saw a quick flash of light. All at once she felt a dreadful chill through her body. There was a moon and it threw shadows down the still, little street. She shivered and wished she was at home, took a deep breath, crossed the empty road and entered the café as Jacques had done.

"Uncle," she said, and gave a rather stout, jolly-looking man dressed in a white apron a kiss on both cheeks. He raised the counter flap and led her into the back room. And there was her Auntie. She was middle-aged, looked very apprehensive and shook hands timidly.

Madeleine's plans had been precisely prepared, and so far everything fitted into place. The smells from the bakery were most agreeable; they reminded her of Chas and Maddy's. Then she forced the very idea out of her mind and conversed as a dutiful niece whom they had not seen for a long time. But they did not stay up long.

Madeleine was shown up a small wooden staircase to a bedroom and, kicking off her shoes, suddenly exhausted, she lay on the bed. She was awakened by noises from the café below; the sun was well up. From a ewer she poured some water into a bowl and splashed it on to her face. Her clothes were creased and ugly but she dismissed this from her mind immediately and creaked lightly down the staircase.

Her Uncle was standing by the counter, as though he had been there all night. They embraced and he told her to sit at one of the tables. There were only four tables in the room. They were small and round, made of pink-streaked marble and supported by black cast-iron filigree tripods. There were three chairs at each table and a few more lined the walls. Uncle brought her some steaming coffee and picking up a couple of white rolls from the counter placed them on to plate before her.

"Bon apetit."

"France in the throes of this ghastly business," she thought, "and my family possibly on the receiving end of a fire-bombing raid." She tried desperately to concentrate on the matter in hand. But the picture kept intruding. "How were her mother and father?" She felt sick and was unable to enjoy the freshly baked rolls. She must try to fix her mind on the brief. It was simple enough. When evening came she was to walk to St. Omer Station, mingle with the crowd of passengers as though she had arrived on the train and return directly to St. Bernard, to her Uncle's café. Frances had asked for every detail of that short journey and Madeleine would have, indelibly to remember them for her report.

She stayed about the house all day and used the french door of the sitting room to reach a small courtyard. In the yard she sat on a bench in the warm sunshine. She felt as though encased in a bubble of unreality. The Uncle was busy in the bakehouse, the Aunt totally engaged with the housework and with the café, and seemed diffident and unwilling to talk to her. Madeleine began to fear the intervening period before she could be active.

A gate led out of the yard onto a back lane. (She and Frances had made this out of thin card!) She peeped out. It must have been siesta. A large cat wrapped itself around her legs. She bent and stroked it. That was the only movement and the silence remained unbroken.

The hours passed slowly and in the evening she had a meal with her Uncle and Aunt. The conversation was awkward and a bit stilted. None of them really knew what to say, and the Uncle was distinctly cagey, almost distrusting of her, she thought. But she could not blame him, if that was how he felt. At sundown she put on her beret and walked to the station. She could have managed the journey blindfold, but she had overlooked the fact that village people pass the time of day.

When she got to the station it was almost dark; the moon had not risen, and she waited for the sound of the distant train approaching. Frances had been absolutely correct; the train from the north was on the far-side track. A few passengers crossed the gantry and made toward St. Omer. Some passengers waited for the train to pull out before crossing the railway line. Madeleine stayed in the shadows and in a few minutes a train approached from the south on the down-side track. It was packed and suddenly the night was full of noise: loud voices and the hissing of the locomotive. Trolleys were being rolled to and from the luggage van as boxes and cases were transferred. She joined the crowd as it headed out of the station. She retraced her steps to St. Bernard. It was remarkable how quickly the crowd had disappeared. Her Uncle was a near-permanent feature at the door of his café. He dutifully kissed his niece and once more lifted the counter flap for her. He did not go with her to the back room and her Aunt who had just sat down after a very busy day pointed to the sofa. Madeleine sat. "First part of the mission accomplished," she thought. "How long shall I have to wait before he gives me his reply and I can get back?"

After a while her Uncle came into the room and beckoned Madeleine to the bar.

"Serve this man please," he said. "I'm busy," and he went to sit at one of the little tables to continue his game of cards.

"Beer, please," said Jacques.

As she tipped the bottle into his glass, he said:

"Be ready at eleven. I will come for you."

She felt reassured by this man's confidence and demeanour.

Her Uncle followed her into the back room and presently gave her an envelope.

"For 'M'," he said.

She waited by the door. The moon was rising and she was startled by Jacque's sudden appearance. He grasped her hand and with great ease got her back to Nieurlet.

She should, of course, have recognised the route they had taken but it all seemed strange and she was glad to put her trust in this man.

Perhaps they had taken a totally different path; she would have to report this to Frances. They stood in the shadow of a hedge.

"Now we have to wait."

He could not see her little smile of recognition.

They waited for more than an hour. She felt cold. Jacques wore a thick black overcoat.

"He's all right," she thought. Then there was the delicious sound of an approaching aircraft engine. Some men standing by the glim-lamps lit them and ran back to the hedge. A Lysander landed, swiftly turned, and taxied back. "Run," said Jacques.

He grabbed her hand, fairly pulled her to the aircraft and shoved her in. Jim lent over and gave Jacques a parcel. No word was spoken, and Madeleine had wanted to say thank you. The whole operation had taken only five minutes; it had been so well practised.

Jim did not follow the river but navigated directly for Hawkinge, steering to the west of Calais.

The glim-lighted runway beneath them now looked to her much like the one they had left behind in France. The landing was smooth and as they taxied to the hangar the glim-lights were extinguished. Jim switched off the engine and did not move for a minute.

"You all right?"

"Yes," she said. "Thank you."

A car came for her later that morning and took her back to Little Gadsden. Danny was waiting for her and almost pounced. She was the most thorough debriefer. She wanted to know details. What had Jacques said? To whom did he give the parcel? What clothes was Uncle wearing? And Auntie? Even did she wear stockings? What colour? And the train on track one, was it on time? And her train; how many passengers? Were they mostly military, did she think? In the café; did he sell bread rolls at the bar; what colour bread? The woman went on and on. Details, details, until Madeleine felt as though she could scream. Some of the questions she could not answer. Danny made a note and returned to them. And finally she said cheerfully "See you at dinner."

There was a note waiting on the dressing table. It read simply: "No damage in Hampstead Road," and was signed E.M. She went to the bathroom, filled the bath extravagantly and unpatriotically with hot water, lay back in it and closed her eyes.

Chapter Forty-Three

On the understanding that nothing of her experience was to be related to anyone, she was given seven days' leave. She had no need of the warning; she had seen enough now to confirm her conviction that the smallest shred of information could be potentially dangerous. She was shocked to see the devastation around her home. The house itself had not been damaged, apart, they said, from a few roof tiles and broken windows. But in Euston Road and around King's Cross the rubble was still being cleared. Dot said that waves of destruction covered the East End and that Chas and Maddy's had again missed the brunt of the bombing.

Leo and Rachel did not change. The business proceeded as usual although they now employed more women. Robert had been called up, had gone very reluctantly and had written once. During her short leave Beccy helped Dot move to a small house in Chalk Farm. She had managed to keep the school open for one morning a week despite the Blitz and had no doubt that, for what it was worth, it would continue for the duration.

Beccy contacted her two students, who seemed remarkably buoyant and well-motivated to succeed in their final examinations, which were imminent. She did very little else that week and spent most of the time at home. She had not realised how physically tired she had become.

It was wonderfully therapeutic to have Rachel to herself all day. Rachel sensed that Beccy would not speak of her work and did not press her. When they were in the kitchen alone they often spoke quietly in German, though never when Leo was about. He was a rock; ran the business well, as Robert had known he would, and did all within his power to give his wife as good a life as times permitted. He delighted in having his daughter home, and they had some quiet and restorative evenings around the kitchen range. They seemed mutually to understand that beneath the crudity and crass stupidity of war delicate situations did arise, and that Beccy was probably engaged in something of this nature. There was a tacit agreement; nothing needed to be verbalised. Beccy was grateful for her parent's discretion.

Chapter Forty-Four

Back at Gadsden Madeleine noticed an almost imperceptible change in the personnel. Danny was unaltered, unless she had become slightly more thorough and dedicated; and one or two of the recruits looked, ironically, more serious and mature. Frances was no longer there, and Danny asked Madeleine to take her place. This was as close as Danny ever came to speaking of rank, and obliquely implied it meant promotion for Madeleine. She had not fully appreciated how hard Frances had worked on her and she felt indebted to her for her dedication. She also came to understand the meaning of the old adage: "If you want to learn a subject, teach it."

She had a man and woman to coach. They studied during the hot summer of 1943, and by autumn all three of them could name every road, canal, bridge and pathway for a five-mile radius around St. Omer. They could also have picked a suitable landing site for a small aircraft around Nieurlet, or named alternative places which would still have given access by foot or bicycle to the town. Although they personally had no direct contact, their organisation kept them informed of the activities of the Resistance with a great amount of local knowledge. Madeleine felt so much better equipped now than she did during her foray to St. Bernard that she wondered how she had managed to come through unscathed. She was also fearful for her two charges and while appreciating the instruction she had received from Frances tried her best to improve upon it. Indeed with better liaison, maps, pictures and information it would have been surprising had she not excelled. And the high standards expected were always kept before them all.

There were lighter moments which helped the long days to pass. They were spared the grosser efforts of The Services Theatrical Agency but for entertainment had an occasional string quartet visit. The music was usually enjoyed, but looking after the players afterwards (they usually had to stay overnight) was strained. There were many reasons for this, but most of the time the inmates no longer felt able to converse in generalities. They had all become rather narrow specialists, except for Danny who, undaunted, was able to deal with all-comers and chatted away affectionately. Occasionally a small dance band would visit, usually led by an elderly man on saxophone, backed by drums and piano. Some of the groups were all-women. When no band was available they sometimes danced to gramophone records. There were liaisons and romances but they were positively discouraged. Madeleine had several mild affairs, and one rather more serious, which involved a Polish student spending the night in her room. This single experience she had not found pleasurable; had regretted its happening and was vigilant in seeing that a similar situation could not recur.

In the late autumn of 1944 Murray arrived at Gadsden and as though it were the most natural opening gambit of conversation advised Madeleine the operation was due to start the following morning. Well, it was a natural outcome; the raison d'être of all the training and detailed rehearsal. As she was being finally briefed, Madeleine found it difficult to quell the fluttering of the butterflies in her stomach. She did not feel this apprehensive last time, she recalled. It did not help when she was told that Jacques would not be available to meet her on this occasion. She was to hand the packet directly into the hands of her Uncle inside the café. If for any reason it could not be given to him in person it was to be burned at the first available opportunity; she knew the procedure.

The early stages of this operation resembled her first. She was vetted by Danny who gave her the sealed packet, contents unspecified, and Madeleine preferred not to guess. She was transported by road to Hawkinge and at night was flown by a pilot to whom she had not been introduced. The landing field was near to Nieurlet. She could almost dream up the contours, she was so well-acquainted with the topography. Almost before the aircraft had come to rest she jumped away. She ran away for cover and had her feet in a ditch before she heard the Lysander take off. In the ensuing silence she was startled by a man who sprang from a hedge and was only slightly mollified when he asked "Madeleine?" He grabbed her hand and pulled her back into the field.

They squatted as a cyclist went past; Madeleine could now see the man beside her. He was fair haired, with a moustache. When their way was clear they crossed the path and took a road which led to the canal. They followed the canal until the tow-path led back to a narrow lane. Some people were approaching, and the man put his arm around Madeleine and began singing obscenely and loud. An elderly couple crossed to the other side of the lane and passed by quickly. The man sobered up immediately and they crossed the canal bridge in silence.

"I leave you here," he said and dissolved into the darkness.

Madeleine found her way easily to the café and was glad no one was about. She pushed open the door and made an undignified entrance as she negotiated a large blanket which hung inside the door to prevent light escaping. Her Uncle put down a tray onto a table and embraced her. Then he returned to the counter and ushered her into the back room. Her Aunt, she understood, was upstairs in bed. The Uncle went back to the café and Madeleine could hear him bolting the door. When he returned he asked abruptly for the packet. She removed it from her clothing and gave it to him. He offered no thanks but indicating the old sofa said she would have to stay there the night, and he immediately returned to the café.

She sat on the sofa and pondered. She had no idea what instructions the packet contained, if indeed they were instructions. She had not expected to be greeted with open arms at one o'clock in the morning but she was surprised at the markedly different attitude of the Uncle from the occasion of her first visit. He had obviously been through a difficult time and he looked much older than she remembered. She did not feel at all tired; in any case she could not sleep and she was hungry. She got to her feet and tapped on the adjoining door. She heard a grunted exclamation and entered. Her Uncle was perusing a small sheaf of note paper. He nodded to her to sit down and continued with his reading. After a few minutes and looking slightly less severe he put the packet of papers into the bottom of an empty beer crate and tossed on top of it a few empty bottles. He offered her a drink which she gladly accepted; and to his surprise asked if she might have a croissant. He sat with her silently while she ate and he realised she was far from tired.

"Do you want to see the bakehouse? I'm just going out."

They went back through the room out into the yard and entered another door further from the house. The smell and the heat were reminiscent of Chas and Maddy's but the sight that met her eyes helped force out this notion. Two boys, who could not have been more than thirteen or perhaps fourteen, skinny as rakes and covered in brown floor dust, were toiling at a large oven. The air was thick with the brown dust. The Uncle said he had not seen much white flour for a year. He called the smaller boy who was pushing dough into a tin and said something to him. The boy left the bakehouse and Uncle continued with the boy's task. Then he reopened the oven and slid in the prepared trays. Madeleine thought it was an absolute inferno and suddenly felt claustrophobic; she must get outside into the air. She turned to leave and caught her arm on the oven's open door. For a split second she could not separate in her mind the fear of being heard from the pain. Then she yelled. The boy rushed to her to see what was wrong. Uncle pushed her toward the sink and allowed cold water to play on her forearm. If not excruciating it was searing, and she stamped her feet to relieve the agony. The cold water gradually reduced the pain and a thick red weal appeared diagonally across her arm. She was glad to get outside.

When she returned to the back room her Auntie was standing there in her long white nightdress. She looked at the wound. Madeleine was shivering. Auntie left and returned almost immediately with a small jar of olive oil. She carefully poured some oil on to the affected arm. Then they both sat down on the old sofa and turned to look at each other. Momentarily, in the silence, it was as though the life-blood of recognition enshrined in generations of womanhood transcended all conscious thought.

"This bloody stupid war," murmured the older woman.

Madeleine said rather feebly: "Please may I come back to see you when it's all over?"

She slept fitfully, mostly in a sitting position. She was certainly awake at dawn and was agreeably surprised that her arm, though swollen, was less painful. When the Aunt came down she wound a clean rag onto the burn. They had very early breakfast together in the café and the young boy from the bakehouse called in to see her before cycling off to his home.

The day was sultry and what sun could be seen seemed to move with deliberate slowness across the sky. She thought she ought not to venture out that day but late in the afternoon she longed for some fresh air and decided to wander down to the canal. The baker-boy, looking even more ghost-like than before, was sitting on the bridge with some friends.

"How's the arm? he called.

"Better," said Madeleine. "And thank you for your help last night. It was silly of me."

She turned and strolled back to the café. She went through the back lane and wondered where the cat had got to. The french window was open and she entered the house.

As the evening drew on a few people came to the café, mostly old men. Madeleine must have been sitting on the sofa for the best part of an hour when a man burst into the room. She recognised him as the person who had met her the previous evening. She did not know his name or his mission but she correctly judged his seriousness. She grabbed her shoulder bag and followed him out into the back lane.

"The youth has been talking," he said.

They were heading toward the canal and as they crossed the bridge they noticed a small van parked in the shadows. The man swung round, grabbed Madeleine's arm which made her squeal and walked straight into three uniformed men who arrested them. As she was bundled into the front seat of the van she heard with horror the man groan with pain as he was thrown into the back. She never saw the man again.

She sat uncomfortably between the driver and his mate as they drove overnight some fifty miles to Lille. The men spoke little and never to her. They smoked Gauloises all the time and she reeked with tobacco smoke and fleetingly remembered Frances forcing a cigarette on to her; it all seemed so long ago. The men had taken her satchel, she was very frightened and as she had only a thin raincoat over her dress, very cold. The moon was rising and she could see the roads were congested with armoured cars, tanks and by general troop movements. There were many diversions and on more than one occasion the van was held for inspection at check-points. Most of the sentries asking questions were German, the driver and his crew were French. They showed their identity cards when asked and explained they had two prisoners on board. At one stop the guards asked for Madeleine's identity card and then the men rummaged through her bag. They presumably searched the man in the back. Whenever the van stopped she could hear him moaning quietly. It must have been about three in the morning when they finally stopped and the man in the back of the van was dragged away into a building.

Not until they had gone inside did the two men release Madeleine. As she stepped down from the vehicle they took her by the arms and entered the building. She was handed over to two women warders who escorted her to a small room. It was not a police cell and Madeleine's first impression was of an improvised lock-up. There was a rough palliasse on the floor, two iron buckets (one containing water), and a chair. The only small window had been wired over. A naked bulb hung from the ceiling. The warders left without speaking and locked the door.

A dreadful silence ensued. She was shivering now as she paced the small room. She tried to collect her thoughts. What had gone wrong? She had tried to puzzle it out during the van ride but to no avail. After all the intensive, agonised training and preparation it had all been reduced to this; she was a prisoner in a foreign country.

Then she had a second to collect her wits as she heard the key turn in the lock. SHE WAS MADELEINE RIBIERRE, NATIVE OF THIS LAND, and she mentally raced through her personal details as a warder came in.

"You have to undress," she said. "Shoes as well."

When Madeleine was naked the women threw her a large heavy linen gown-like garment which she put on. The warder stuffed Madeleine's clothes into an old cardboard box and left. Madeleine remained standing and tried to summon her resources. This was the usual procedure before interrogation, she rehearsed. The gown was prickly and smelled sour. It enveloped her from neck to ankles and felt heavy. But it did provide some warmth and she stopped shivering.

Where was she? Interrogation would probably not come for a few hours, offer of food would be most unlikely; she would call out for a drink of water or if she wanted the lavatory.

She was a French citizen going about her lawful business when this thug grabbed her and by association she had been wrongfully arrested. No charge had been made. She tried to explain to her captors during the van journey but they were not interested, wouldn't listen. Yes, she was ready with a plan of action and this slightly lessened the tension.

She sat down on the palliasse trying to conserve her energy, and held her feet in her hands under the heavy linen. She must have dozed longer than she imagined. A shaft of light cast through the window; the early morning sun. She summoned all her will, determined on a ploy which she thought would be a positive step towards her release. She hammered with her fists on the door and shouted. First she yelled she wanted the lavatory and when she received no answer she repeated the request in a cruder vein. She screamed to be let out; what right had they to detain her? Then she screamed she had been kidnapped and wanted her lawyer. This was met with silence and she repeated the performance while trying not to damage her knuckles on the door.

Later that morning two women came in and marched her to a desk in the outer office. A uniformed man asked her some questions as though she had reported a lost animal. She said she knew her rights, where were her clothes, she had been kidnapped and would be making a report to the authorities. The man at the desk looked at her witheringly, told her to shut up, and they knew exactly who she was and what she was up to. Madeleine continued to protest; the warders took her back to the lock-up while she loudly demanded the lavatory. They slung her in this time and retreated hastily.

She had been warned in training to try to keep some idea of the time of day. Like so much else in Special Operations this had sounded quite plausible at Gadsden. In the field it was always more complicated. She had calculated that the window had an easterly aspect and could see the sun was about as high as it would get. Probably about noon now. She had not eaten since early yesterday morning. They were bound to give her something within the next six hours.

In this surmise she was partly correct. It must have been early afternoon when she was taken out by one woman who held her arm tightly causing her damaged arm to sting. They went in the opposite direction from the office, to a long low room which looked drab and dingy. It had one table with a chair on each side. She had entered at one end and she noticed there was a door at the other. She was told to sit by the woman guard who then retreated to the door by which they had entered. Presently a genial bald-headed man entered. His French was good, with a slight German accent. Madeleine thought he was from the Ruhr or had learned French at school which had become polished by usage. He bid her good afternoon, asked her name, address, age, business in St. Omer and apologised for having 'pulled her in.' He knew she was only a pawn, he said, but they were having too much trouble with the Resistance these days. He had no time for the Resistance, he said. They were not going to shorten the war or make it any easier for France to survive afterwards.

"Would you like some food?" He clapped his hands and a uniformed man entered behind him. "Coffee and fruit!" he said, and the man left immediately.

The bald one continued amiably. They had picked up several men claiming to be "Free French" and they were bringing some more in tonight. It would make it easier for him and much better for her if she could give him a couple of names, then she would be free to go.

"I don't know any of them," said Madeleine. "That man just grabbed me as I happened to be standing near."

"But, M'amselle, you were seen running with some men. Please do not waste time. I have a meeting to go to, and I am sure you want to get back home."

Madeleine changed tack slightly, and then wished she hadn't. "I don't know any names. That's the truth."

Some biscuits and a cup of coffee were put on to the table. Madeleine's stomach was in knots.

"A couple of names and you're out of here," he said.

She repeated her statement.

"Have some biscuits," he said evenly.

As she reached for the coffee he caught her hand.

"Just one name and we can all go home."

She sipped the coffee slowly but did not replace the mug until it had been drained. She hurriedly took another biscuit as he removed the plate.

137

"Think about it," he said, "I'll see you in a few days time." He called to the warder who had remained at the far end of the room. As she left he said again; "A few days time."

She did then lose her grip on the passage of time. She found a piece of bread on a tin plate and an empty mug beside her on the floor. She must have slept; she had no memory of anyone entering or leaving. She crumbled the bread and ate it slowly, but could not fancy dipping the mug into the bucket of water.

She was again taken into the interrogation room and the procedure with the bald one went very much as before. He was perhaps a little less patient with her, but called for coffee and watched while she drank. He gave the impression that he was very anxious to get this little episode cleared up. Again he asked for names. Again he added that just one name would solve their problem. Finally he expressed the view which Madeleine immediately recognised as the classic approach.

He said conspiratorially: "It's all been a horrible mistake. You should never have been arrested. Please give me a name, I can sign the release warrant and you can go back to your Auntie's."

Madeleine was feeling weak and repeated she knew no names and she should be released.

"Of course you do. Who wants to be stuck in a place like this? I'm sure I don't."

He looked at her encouragingly. There was a moment's silence then he called the warder. She ambled forward as though she too was thoroughly fed up, grabbed Madeleine's arm and escorted her back to the lock-up.

Madeleine tried screaming for attention and demanding to speak to a solicitor. Her voice was thin and did not carry. She leant against the wall, but now her legs could no longer take her weight and she sank to the floor. When she awoke her eyes felt gravelly, her throat sore, her limbs were aching and she had a temperature. She could not get to her feet. Her gown was stinking and she was disgusted. She found it difficult to hold two thoughts together and for a moment thought she was probably out of her mind. She managed to crawl across to the bucket and she rinsed her mouth with water, then she lay flat and looked at the ceiling. There was bound to be further interrogation. She knew no names and being in a state of near-delirium would probably reveal her own identity. She retained enough professionalism though to know that the sessions so far had been the softening-up process and that the next one would probably involve the 'hard man.'

The door was being unlocked and she braced herself as best she could but she could not stand. The warder called over her shoulder and eventually two of them got her to the chair for interrogation. The warders moved to the back of the room and Madeleine could hear their faint grumblings. She had not even the strength to sit, but slumped on the chair with her head on her arms across the table. Some minutes passed when she heard the unmistakable voice of the bald one speaking in German. All she caught was "...... this piffling affair, for God's sake."

She heard him leave and squinted to see her new persecutor. He was still standing back in the shadow but she noticed he had a mop of red hair. He came toward her and scraped the chair as he sat. Something forced her to look up. An electric shock flashed through her whole body; for a split second she sat bolt upright in the chair then her head flopped almost lifeless to the table. All the interrogator could see of her was a scalp of matted black hair. She mumbled something and to hear what was said he put his hand on the table, his ear close to her head. She could not get her muscles to work; could not get her tongue around the word "George." She covered his hand with hers and whispered the one word "Dresden." He moved his hand away quickly. He could not hear what she said.

"What's that?"

She tried again but her mouth would not form the one word she most wanted to say.

"Speak up," he said.

She tried to raise her head but could not. He put his head close again. Straining every nerve in her wracked body she said: "Dresden vases."

What his inner reaction was she could not tell, but he put his hand under her chin and lifted her face.

"Gott in Himmel."

He gently let her head down on to the table and stood up. He called to the warders at the back of the room to disappear. They needed no second bidding and left immediately. He held her hand and lifted her chin.

"Listen! please listen," he whispered. "Can you hear?"

She barely nodded.

"The man brought in with you gave a name yesterday; Marcel Crouchon, from Bethune. Can you hear me?" He was frantic. "Say it, say Marcel Crouchon."

She tried to move her lips but couldn't. He put his mouth near to her face.

"Mouth this, 'M-a-r-c-e-l-C-r-o-u-c-h-o-n.'" He tried it slowly letter by letter.

At last her lips moved enough to give him a glimmer of hope. He put his hand softly on her matted head and for a second she felt some kind of peace. Then she realised how petrified he was and how he had to struggle to move away from her. He called out for the warders. He did not recognise his own voice and moving quickly toward the door called again. The two women eventually slouched in and carried Madeleine back to the lock-up.

Chapter Forty-Five

She was lying on the palliasse when she regained consciousness. She had a sore throat. She wondered whether she was delirious. It was surely akin to delirium. As she tried to organise her thoughts she saw a mug of coffee on the floor. She sat up with great difficulty and sipped. It was stone cold and watery but it eased her throat. When at last her head stopped spinning she found her mind focusing on George's face. Then she saw him testing the smoothness of the porcelain against his cheek. She felt his head close to hers. Her lips were trying to form words. She finished the coffee. She was certainly weak but felt as though the fever had left her.

Had she seen George? Had he been trying to tell her something? Was he in this building? With a strength she did not know she had she scrambled to her feet and banged on the door calling his name. She called and called until in utter exhaustion she sagged to the floor.

She was no longer conscious of any passage of time and was aware only of being roughly handled by the two women who were dragging her down the corridor. She was hoisted on to the chair and her head and shoulders flopped on to the table.

She did not even have the energy to despair, certainly not sufficient reserve to reflect for a fleeting second on her disciplined training. She could hear the interrogator entering and knew his identity by the way he cleared his throat. He began by wishing 'Mam'selle Ribierre Good morning,' and was obviously unaware he had kindled the faintest spark of hope in his prisoner's mind by that salutation. She registered that he, at least, did not know her identity.

He bent forward and leaning toward her said,

"The heavy mob are moving in tomorrow. I shall be gone thank God. Away from this hole." He said with some feeling, "you could be away too."

She could hardly hear his voice over the throbbing of her head but she felt he wanted to convey to her how fair he had been.

"Just one name to wind it all up."

He went through the food and drink routine again and when she had drained the mug he applied pressure.

"Your Uncle and Aunt are now in great danger. Invasion by the Allied Troops is imminent. It's most unlikely that any more time will be spent on petty tribunals like this. You will be shipped off to Germany. And there, my girl, you will sink without trace. Believe me!"

He went droning on and on and eventually the last shred of Madeleine's will-power snapped. She whispered something. He leaned forward to hear her.

"What?" he said. "Say it louder!"

Without moving her jawbone she said: "Crouchon."

"What?" he kept saying. "What? Speak up a bit."

"Crouchon," she said it quite clearly. Marcel Crouchon."

She looked up and saw his face register disgust and disappointment in equal proportion. She felt that had he been less of a gentleman he would have spat at her. He stormed out leaving no instruction to the warders. After a few minutes they sauntered forward and part carrying, part dragging, deposited her back on to the palliasse.

She did not see them go or hear the door being locked. It did not register with her how long the interval was but she became aware of a movement beside her. A warder had her arm around her. They were both sitting on the floor. Before her was a cardboard box which she eventually focused on as containing her clothes.

"I'll help you dress," said the woman. She stripped off the filthy gown and reached inside the box.

Madeleine crawled forward and sat by the bucket. She splashed some water on to her body. The warder left her and returned in a moment with a huckaback roller towel. It was not very dry and not very clean but she dabbed the girl's body and gradually got her into her clothes.

Madeleine could barely stand. The warder took her arm and eased her toward the office. She was given her satchel and a travel warrant for St. Omer. She was asked to sign. The officer at the desk dipped the pen in the ink and handed it to her. She was to sign to say she had received her belongings intact and for the warrant. She could hardly feel the pen in her hand and she automatically made a preparatory down-stroke for a capital "R." She fumbled with the scratchy nib and made the stroke adapt to an "M." "M. Ribierre," she signed painfully. Then she just stood there.

The warder put the sling of the satchel over Madeleine's shoulder and looked at her face. She pushed fifty centimes into her hand and told her to go. Madeleine could not move. The woman put her arm around her and guided her to the door she had entered that fateful night; how long ago? She could barely place one foot in front of the other. In the umbrella rack by the door was a disowned knobkerry walking stick. The warder snatched it up quickly and thrust it into the girl's hand. Madeleine hobbled out bent and slow, leaning on the stick.

She followed her nose dragging her stick along the pavement. The smell from a café overpowered her. She entered and flopped onto the nearest chair. A girl waitress, about twelve years old, came to her and returned with a bowl of potage and some bread. Madeleine dipped the bread into the soup and took a long time to eat. People came and went. Some murmured "Bon apetit" as they passed. The room was full of tobacco smoke and the heavy garlic fumes from the cooking. She could not appreciate the passage of time but she was aware that the door bell had clanged many times before her plate was empty. She waved feebly for the waitress and was given a bill she had to hold close to her eyes to read. Then she tried her legs. All she wanted to do was sleep. She struggled to her feet and asked the way to the station. The girl pointed with one hand and in the other held out the walking stick. Madeleine thanked her and asked her to keep it. The girl shrugged her shoulders and leant it against the wall.

Chapter Forty-Six

By the time Madeleine reached the station it was nightfall. It was a dismal picture. The station was so packed with uniformed troops that some of them found they were being pushed from the trackside on to the rails. It was the usual mixture of humanity. Some of the soldiers were loud and bawdy, some quiet, some eating from knapsacks, drinking from bottles, lighting cigarettes which suddenly flared their faces in the dark, some with their arms around each other and some she tripped over as they sat on their kitbags.

The train was late, hours late. When it did arrive there was no order, no boarding sergeant, just a surge forward; not a stampede but a slow and solid mass imperceptibly edging toward the train. Madeleine was lifted up the steps and she stood crammed into a corridor. She could not feel her feet; dreamed of levitation and was held in some kind of suspended animation. The train eventually moved and the wall of bodies settled like sediment.

She could hardly breathe. A soldier pressed against her eating a bread roll. He must have held it in his mouth while boarding the train, she thought, he could never have got his hands down to pocket level. She tried not to dismiss these petty diversions from mind. She didn't even mind the crush, it was warm at last and she proved the theory that sleep could easily be achieved in the upright position. Like the campaigners surrounding her she imagined that for them all time had become a new dimension. She could not hazard a guess at the time of day; certainly did not know which day it was, but the gradual onset of dawn began to change the shape of the corridor.

She did not feel quite so well supported now and looking down she saw some men sleeping in a pile on the floor. She struggled to move her feet but they were wedged. A man near her managed to swig from a bottle. He passed it to her and she drank some tepid water. The train stopped and she heard the word Hazebrouk running around. Some of the troops alighted and for the first time she was able to see that there were a few civilians among the passengers. No railway guard appeared and the train eventually started agin. There was now a bit more room to move. An officer opened his case, unwrapped some meat and bread, and offered some to Madeleine. She accepted and ate a small portion very slowly. Becoming aware of her appearance she was startled and admired the man who shared his food with a dishevelled refugee. He had left his spot now and she saw him find a corner in which he huddled over his meal.

When the train arrived at St. Omer she had to ask some soldiers to lift her down. She was embarrassed but could not get her legs to work. When she was deposited beside the track they asked if she was all right. She said she would be. Presently she edged her way to the barrier, it was open and no one asked for a ticket. The crowd had thinned out by the time she hobbled into the street. She was bent almost double, her clothes were ragged and the thought crossed her mind that she was probably less conspicuous now than she had been all those months ago when, quite neatly dressed, she had mingled with the crowd leaving the down platform.

Painfully slowly she made her way to St. Bernard. She entered the back lane, stood by the gate, looked down at her feet and again wondered where the cat was. She approached the french window and found it unlocked. Closing it quietly behind her she sank down on to the sofa. She could not have been there long when she felt a hand shaking her shoulder.

"Wake up, wake up!" said the voice.

She groaned and tried to turn over. She was irritated by the shaking and longed for sleep. She opened her eyes to slits and gradually focused on the face of a woman she recognised. She continued to be shaken.

"You can't stay here."

Eyes wide open now to danger she saw the Aunt.

"Wake up, you must go!"

Madeleine's eyes closed again, she seemed to have no control over the weights on her eye-lids. Then all was black and perfect peace. Again the agonising interruption. She felt her feet being rubbed. Her Aunt had put some soup and a bread roll by the sofa.

"You can't stay here," she said more fearfully than urgent.

The bell clanged in the café. She propped Madeleine up to reach the soup and left her. She returned after some minutes and pushed a pair of thick stockings on to the girl's legs. Madeleine's eyes opened wearily, she crumbled the bread roll into the soup which had become cold and wiped the plate clean. The older woman did not take her eyes from her. She kept repeating the same few words.

"You must not stay."

She left for the café again at the summons of the bell. Madeleine heard a hubbub of voices and a cloud of strong tobacco smoke seeped in. When the Aunt returned she climbed the staircase and brought down a long-sleeve woolly jumper. She removed Madeleine's raincoat and pulled the jumper over her head, threading her skinny arms into the sleeves as though dressing a child.

"You must leave here as soon as I tell you. Please sit up. Now, can you stand?"

Madeleine stood, by bracing her calf muscles against the sofa and then after balancing for a few seconds sat down again. The woman went back into the café and returned with a few bread rolls and a bottle of beer in her pockets. She pushed the provisions into Madeleine's satchel. Madeleine was more conscious now and found her voice. In little more than a breathy squeak she asked where her Uncle was.

The older woman put her hands to her face and after a while said simply "He is not here." She turned and hurried into the café.

Madeleine put on her raincoat, sat and waited and, despite a conscious struggle to keep awake, lolled sideways and slept.

She awoke to a darkened room. She was being shaken again. She felt desperate. She would kill the person depriving her of sleep. She knew how to. Pierre had taught her. Stab the knife! Somebody, a man by the smell, was saying; "Come now!" It was Jacques. He took her hand and pulled, then with his arm around her waist hoisted her out, through the french window, across the courtyard and out of the gate into the lane. The cold night air struck her face; she pulled her beret over her ears and looked at Jacques. He said nothing, but bent down and hauled her on to his back. He was built like an ox. She was featherweight and he crossed the canal bridge and some fields carrying her easily. But after climbing a ridge he puffed with the extra exertion. At the top they saw the moon rising and paused for a rest. Nearby was a barn, he opened the great creaky gate and deposited her on to a stook of hay: the hay smelled sweet and new.

He spoke. "We can stay here tonight without danger." They would have to stay put all the next day. That would present difficulties, but if all went well he would get her to a safe house the following night. He pulled a horse blanket from a rafter and covered her with it. Madeleine could but wonder. She and Jacques had met only briefly before and yet she had taken his help for granted. She held his rough hand.

"Thank you," she said. He bent forward and kissed her forehead.

Daybreak came with the sounds of the farm waking up. Jacques heaved Madeleine up some wooden steps to the hay loft.

"Don't make a sound."

He left her hidden in the back of the barn. He must have been gone an hour or more and when he returned he had a billy-can of hot coffee. She opened her bag, took out the rolls and while they were eating she handed him the bottle of beer which he put into the deep pocket of his coat.

"They are trying to find a suitable landing strip," he said as though he were concluding a long conversation.

Her voice had gained more strength. She asked;

"Why a safe house?"

He almost looked through her when he said that the allied forces invasion was imminent and now, in many ways, things were more difficult for him, and by deduction for her, than they had been before. They would have to bide their time and be especially vigilant. Madeleine wondered how many service-men in the field had a grasp of current affairs to match Jacques.

The day passed without incident. They were not discovered, or perhaps the local farmer was as aware of the position as Jacques. At all events when night came she was able to walk and after about two hours of stumbling they arrived at a very small house which seemed to be their destination. It was tumble-down. There were a couple of very old arm chairs in one room and in the adjoining room there was a sink with a single dripping tap. Jacques said he would be back and left her. A beam of moonlight penetrated the taped-up window glass.

Madeleine tried the tap. It obliged with a slightly more persistent drip. She filled her mouth with water and rubbed her teeth with a finger. She rearranged her clothes and tried to rid herself of the wisps of hay. And for the first time for many days she tried to take stock. Had she spoken to George? Not a dream? She shivered. She could still smell the stinking gown that had covered her. The interrogator's voice haunted her: "Just one name, just one name." What was George doing? Where was he now?

"George." She called his name in the darkness. The dripping tap recalled her, but her mind was now teeming. What had happened to the Uncle? Though she had delivered the papers to him it looked as though the whole operation had been a fiasco. She had a slightly clearer head now and mouthed "Dresden vases."

"What does that mean?" said Jacques who had just returned.

She swung round alarmed. Then relaxed when she saw him.

"It's only a code," she said.

He plopped into one of the chairs and lay asleep as she watched him. She was sentinel now. He had brought more coffee, in a tin flask this time, and it was still quite warm. She drank some and screwed the lid back tightly. She gauged the whereabouts of this house and its proximity to a possible landing strip. And still feeling quite weak she sat in the other chair and dozed on and off.

The sun was fairly high when Jacques began to rouse. He drank some coffee and lit a cigarette.

"Listen!" he said. "They can no longer risk bringing in an aircraft. I should be getting another message tonight. Maybe they'll try to arrange a boat."

"What?" Her voice was quite shrill. He looked up at the uncharacteristic sound.

"I am out of my depth now. If they want you on the north coast I can only point you in the right direction."

The daylight hours dragged by. He had food which they shared. He was obviously not far from his source of supply, she thought.

When at long last darkness came, he left saying he would be back in the early morning. Now she felt desolate and wretched. She stripped, washed from the dripping tap, shook her clothing and although fatigued felt slightly better in spirit, which did not last long. She sat in the chair, covered herself with her raincoat and tried to imagine herself away from here. She felt she hardly knew who was herself. Here was a youngish woman sitting and sleeping at every opportunity. Her immediate past was a nightmare and she found it difficult to separate reality from the dream.

When Jacques returned he sat deep in the chair, looked at her for a second or two and then with his chin inside his greatcoat closed his eyes. The time dragged for Madeleine and it was noon before he stirred. He delved into his pockets and brought out a lettuce. Without washing it they ate the leaves with some bread and drank cold coffee. They were sitting on the old chairs facing each other.

"They are going to try to pick you up by boat. In two days' time, at high tide, which is about one o'clock in the morning. The place they have chosen is just south of Hardelot Plage. I went there once as a child; played on the beach; have not been there since. It's quite out of my area. I will see you part of the way."

"Jacques," she said, quietly and deliberately after a pause, "I cannot do it." She knew from memory of the map study at Gadsden that it must lie some forty miles to the west, near Le Touquet.

The man looked at her and said nothing. He reached for her satchel which lay on the floor between them and opened it. He withdrew a piece of paper, her travel warrant to St. Omer, scrutinised it, put it in his pocket and dropped the bag on to the floor.

She did not move.

That night he left her again and when he returned at dawn showed her two railway warrants for the journey from St. Omer to Samer. He said they would have to change at Desvres and that they should try to catch the train that evening. He said he would have to sleep and she should prepare for the journey. She wondered what preparations she could make and tried to project her mind toward the proposed route.

If they got as far as Samer it would leave a distance of some ten miles to the sea. The beach would be protected by barbed wire; it would be dark; she could not do it.

Jacques got up and stretched. It was late afternoon. They set off and when they reached the town he put his arm around her and they made their way to the down-line at the station.

The train was late coming in. They had some coffee and rolls in a café; it was quite dark when the engine steamed in from the south. The train was already full but they managed to squeeze into the corridor. They had not been asked to show their tickets. The train trundled slowly and took two hours to get to Desvres. They had to wait another two hours for a connection by local train to Samer. Then they were asked to show their warrants and were cheerfully waved through to a sidings-entrance. The local train was fairly well on time. It was a non-corridor but they still had to stand. The little train puffed and rattled its way slowly round the bends until it came to a squeaky halt. Judging by the exodus most of the passengers must have alighted; they pushed out with the crowd and found the road for Neufchatel.

They walked steadily along the roadside, their shadows from the moonlight cast before them. After a while they branched away toward Hameau-Du-Chemin and could smell the sea. They entered a forested area where they decided they should rest up for the night. They collected some fallen pine cones and bracken with which they covered their legs and huddled together. Jacques did his best to visualise a plan, but as he had said, this neck of the woods was outside his experience.

This temporary encampment was little more than a mile from the sea, and he was impatient to move on. They moved away from the trees then and stopped again in a little copse overlooking the beach by Mont St. Frieux. The moon was now high and the shoreline clear. The place was quiet and deserted, not a soul in sight. They moved down to the dunes and as they had feared came across a barbed wire barricade. Jacques found one of the heavy timber supporting tripods, draped his coat across the wire close to the frame and climbed to the top. He lay on his side and heaved Madeleine up after him. They balanced together on the top for a moment then he lifted her over the wire and pushed her forward. She landed on the sand, he dropped by her and then scrambled back for his coat. They stood together and realised they were bleeding from jagged cuts on their arms and legs. He put on his torn greatcoat and looked out to sea. It was calm, the waves only gently toppling over. Judging by the seaweed line it was not quite high tide. If no boat appeared before dawn they would have to renegotiate the barbed wire. Apart from the gentle surf there was not a sound to be heard.

It was becoming cold and he opened his coat and enveloped Madeleine. She had her face on his thick tweed coat which smelled strongly of tobacco. From the protection of his coat she turned and scanned the water line. He thought he saw lights but it was the moon reflecting on the crests as they broke near the shore. So gently, he planted a kiss on her head. This was suspended animation made flesh. Then quietly she said; "I live in Hampstead Road, London. Will you tell me your name?"

He turned her head softly in his hands. "Well, it really is Jacques. Jacques ....."

He did not finish the sentence. Without warning dark figures surprised them. They saw one man carried a sub-machine gun which was directed at the single silhouette. Madeleine broke loose from Jacques without realising the danger and felt the sharp nozzle of a gun in her ribs.

"Woss your name?" demanded a distinctly Cockney voice. "And 'oos this?!

"Madeleine Ribierre," she said. "This is my friend."

"Get on the ground mate!" said the voice. "Move and I'll blow your 'ed off."

One man grabbed the girl and dragged her away. With the gun pointed at the recumbent Jacques the man kept him covered as he retreated backwards guided by the third man. They waded into the water. It rose to Madeleine's neck before she felt herself being roughly manhandled aboard. The three men were then heaved up and the small boat immediately put out to sea. It was all over in a couple of minutes.

The crossing was without incident for Madeleine. She had been given hot tea and blankets and was left by herself in the small cabin below. She was put ashore at Folkestone and it was still dark when she found herself in a hospital having the abrasions to her arms and legs attended.

The following morning she was put on a train to Charing Cross, accompanied by an ATS girl who kept fussing and trying to keep her wrapped up warmly. She was taken by taxi to a military hospital near Victoria Station, again examined and given a bed in a single ward. Far from feeling grateful Madeleine wanted to die. She was given an injection and she slept.

She had no idea for how long; it might have been days. A woman doctor was talking to her as she woke. They were treating the abrasions on her legs and arms. There was also an outbreak of small boils on her back which would probably take quite a long time before they responded to treatment.

"You will have to undergo a course of injections," the doctor said. "It looks as though you will be with us for a fortnight."

The girl looked at the doctor in disbelief as though she had never before heard the word "fortnight."

She was told that a visitor would be with her soon, and it did not seem long before Danny appeared. Madeleine recalled every detail as exactly as possible, thinking she had left out nothing other than the identification of one interrogator. Anyway, she was not sure herself. Then Danny, with a cheerful smile, started over again.

"How did you come by two travel warrants? Were they made or purchased over the counter? Who made them? Where were they made?" She knew exactly where the boat had beached. "How far away were they when they were found? Three hundred yards? Less? What was the exact location of Jacques' safe-house?"

When that was mentioned Madeleine pulled the sheet over her head and said "Go away." Quite distinctly.

Danny left at once, and at the door paused and called cheerfully: "See you tomorrow!"

Danny must have stayed in town overnight. Madeleine's dressings had only just been replaced when she saw her enter. Danny beamed.

"Good morning dear," she presented Madeleine with a huge bunch of chrysanthemums. Madeleine was sitting on the side of the bed, her bandaged legs showing. Danny asked politely about her medical condition and treatment but could not for long sustain this mode and soon got down to business. She began asking questions again. This time she wanted chronology.

"Why were you given the name Marcel Crouchon? What happened to him?"

"I don't know," Madeleine said.

"Try to think. Describe the second interrogator to me again."

Madeleine did her best and had to improvise around the one small part she did not wish to recount.

"Tell me that again. Was he wearing uniform?"

"No!" she nearly screamed. She felt like blaspheming into a long unbroken shout, but she described him as required and then had to suffer pins and needles in her head.

Danny said "Your parents have been notified, and they are coming to see you tomorrow. I'll let you rest now and pop in again this afternoon, if I may," she added rhetorically.

That afternoon a third party might have been forgiven for thinking Madeleine and Danny, though the best of friends, had not met for years. The woman was an absolute glutton; she absorbed the details, came up for more and looked stronger with the passage of time. Madeleine withered eventually under the onslaught, but she had been well trained, had a strong constitution and was able to withhold one simple piece of information.

Whether Danny was satisfied could not be detected. She gave Madeleine a hug and left. There was the characteristic parting shot at the door. "I'll pop in next week."

Oh God, thought Madeleine and gave her a weary smile.

Leo and Rachel came the next afternoon. They were naturally quiet and comforting and so familiar that really they did very little talking. They sat on chairs with their knees nearly touching. Beccy realised that no words could express their profound relief.

"Joe sends his love and will be down to see you. We have had letters from Tom and from Robert and from Dot. She is satisfied with her new house and still teaches one day a week and says to tell you your two students have passed with flying colours."

Beccy was floating away on these affectionately-offered platitudes but they did not afford any lasting sense of relief.

Danny returned as promised, five days later. She had been to the War Office, she said by way of introduction. But her questions this visit were less specified; only generally directed. Beccy sensed she knew more than she was prepared to reveal. Come to that, she thought, 'This woman rarely reveals anything.

"When you are discharged from here the M.O. should grant you twenty-one days' leave."

It was a very short visit. She stood to leave.

When she paused at the door Beccy was expecting the usual cheery 'See you soon,' but she just smiled and said no more. Beccy experienced a strong feeling of finality as though a phase of her life had ended.

She recuperated very quickly and was discharged from the hospital after only six days. She had not been able to get a message out in time so no one came to meet her. This, she did not mind at all. She carried a small bag and wearing a beautifully laundered dress walked out into the spring sunshine. The women drivers swept their buses in and out of Victoria Station just as though the world had never stopped. She would love to have walked but feeling shaky she boarded a number twenty-nine and enjoyed the ride.

The house at Hampstead Road stood solid and she thought quite defiant. She tapped on the window and Leo came to the door. The old kitchen and the candlelit suppers had lost none of their charms. Leo and Rachel were as loving and considerate as usual. Joe had cycled down to London and Beccy was delighted to see him. Yet, surrounded by all this security she could confide her deepest anxiety to no one. She wrote immediately to Bernadette in Dublin and within a few days received a reply. Beccy should come as soon as possible. A week after leaving hospital she was on her way to Ireland.

Chapter Forty-Seven

Bernadette opened the door to her, and the two women held both hands out in greeting. For a moment they looked at each other. Bernadette was, if anything more beautiful than ever and her aura of worldly maturity engulfed the younger woman. They clasped each other as though they perfectly understood all the nuances of human emotion.

Bernadette said quietly,

"He's in the drawing room," and pointed to the door.

Beccy entered and saw him sitting in an armchair. He turned his head, smiled and held out his hands. Beccy went slowly toward him and knelt by his side. How he had changed! In only a few weeks. He looked much older, no longer any trace of boyishness, his complexion shallow, cheeks pinched and unshaven. She put her head against his chest and he laid his hands on to her hair. Neither could have said for how long they stayed in this one position. They did not speak or move. Every fibre of their bodies responded and a healing process, denied to them for so long, began to permeate their being.

George had difficulty standing. His left foot had been crushed and the leg was set in plaster. He was receiving treatment for nervous disability but was hindering his recovery by drinking too much alcohol.

"The day after you went, the Germans pulled out. Off course I had to travel with them. I was looking for a chance to escape. When the convoy slowed down I jumped from the cab and caught a foot under the wheel of a following vehicle. The convoy did eventually stop but they had covered a distance of about fifty yards, by which time I had rolled into a ditch. They did make a perfunctory search but it was dark and they were in a hurry to move off."

George continued with his story. He had not told Bernadette and the women listened with set faces.

"Eventually I staggered into a farm near to Noyelles and made contact with the Resistance. I was lucky."

Beccy held his hand. He was trembling. The rest of the story would have to wait for another time. There was no hurry now. Bernadette left them together on the settee. When she returned she gently draped a blanket around their shoulders, observed them lovingly and took herself to bed.

The following evening, after dinner, Beccy and Bernadette left George with a friend at the table and adjourned to the drawing room. Neither of them wanted any coffee; the night was drawing in and they walked in the garden where they spent only a few minutes. They returned to the house and began to recall old times. They remembered the name and location of the hotel in Germany where before the war they had laid plans to extend their business. Bernadette told Beccy about some of the decisions she had to make in the Civil Service. George, she said, had become an agent in the Secret Service. Most of the time he spent operating in Germany, but as you know only too well, latterly near the French border. She knew no more about his work than that.

"When did you first know of this?" Beccy asked.

Bernadette stood up and made her way to the kitchen. She had changed her mind; she would have some coffee after all.

'When did you first know?" Beccy repeated.

Bernadette put some coffee cups on to the table and reached some saucers from the open dresser.

"I was sworn to secrecy when I came back to Dublin. It could have endangered his life."

"But why didn't you tell me?" she said angrily. "Why didn't you tell me?"

There was no answer. Beccy could see from Bernadette's face that she knew she had hurt, possibly irretrievably damaged, the relationship she most cherished. Only an hour earlier Beccy had thought her feet were at long last on solid foundations and that she would be able, with George's help, to rebuild their lives. She went back, out into the garden. It was chill and dark and she returned quickly to the drawing room.

George's friend rose as she entered. George patted the seat of a chair inviting her to come near him. After a while the companion said he would go and see what Bernadette was up to. With the aid of crutches George swung himself on to the settee. Beccy sat close. He put his arm around her and they sat in the enveloping quiet of the night.

Next morning George took her to his own room in this rambling house.

"You should just see it in the morning light," he said.

No beams from the sun entered the room but the pale blue ceiling evenly distributed the northern light. She had never seen such a gloriously sedate room. The wall hangings and the pictures reflected his taste and discernment. For a second she recalled his flat in Berlin, but was glad to escape the thought. Here, the walls were painted white and in one corner of the room stood an open three-sided cupboard made of old discoloured pine and crowned with a dome. Housed under the canopy stood a pair of Dresden vases. In that setting they were noble, elegant, simply beautiful; and spoke directly to her heart. She was mesmerised, could not remove her gaze.

George turned his head towards Beccy, "Remember them? They are yours."

With all the travelling involved Beccy had only three full days in Dublin. George and she were inseparable for that short period. He was, in many ways, far more psychologically damaged than she. It was apparent he had been under great strain for many months and the recent bouts of heavy drinking had not helped the healing process. Beccy felt herself to be well on the road to recovery and was beginning to savour life in Ireland, helping George to regain his confidence. But time had run out.

Owing to his inability to walk far he had not come to the station. In her heart she did not know whether she could forgive Bernadette for not confiding in her. She felt wounded by having had to suffer the long period of doubt. She thought she would never be able to forget the hollow frustration and uncertainty when she had not heard from Bernadette or George. She was sufficiently philosophical, however, to recognise that many people had suffered in this way during the past few years.

Bernadette hugged her when they parted at the station and implored her to return as soon as possible.

"He needs you."

Chapter Forty-Eight

Beccy had to make a very quick turnaround at home and spent only one night there, enough to catch up with the latest news. She did not see Dot, and Joe was unable to get down from Hatfield owing to pressure of work. Tom was still in the north, very uncommunicative except that he wanted to get home. The good news was that Robert had been commissioned. He was a born leader, as they knew. He had risen through the ranks quickly, had completed the Officer Corps Training Course and was now in the eighth army and at the time of writing was on a short leave in Egypt.

Beccy was not looking forward to Gadsden. There was some kind of disorientation in her mind and she had to recheck her calendar to appreciate she had been absent for little more than six weeks. Danny was as ever, bubbling with all the latest developments. All the familiar faces greeted her as a long lost relative, but the membership had altered over her absence and it seemed as though the atmosphere of the place had changed; almost imperceptibly.

The long-awaited invasion of France had taken place and its effects reverberated around the whole world. Yet at Gadsden there was a sensation of low morale. To the agents of the S.O.E. this was not particularly ironic; their days of usefulness were numbered. They were, of course, glad the end was in sight, but there were agonies of withdrawal to be endured. The better motivated members were wondering how they would cope with demobilisation, and the foreign staff concerned about whether they would have a home to go back to. It was a bewildering time for the so-called non-combatants.

Beccy had a fresh person to teach. She did her best, but encourage as she might, any ingredient of immediacy was lacking. In the late autumn of 1944 she was granted indefinite leave and told to phone in once each week, a procedure which previously had been strongly discouraged. She bade farewell to Danny and left for London.

Letters were awaiting her. She first read one from George. It was more than a month old, as mail had not been allowed in either direction while she was on duty. She smiled as she read and knew they would be reunited soon. Bernadette's letter, dated only a few days ago, said simply that George was in hospital. Could she join them soon? Beccy imagined he was having surgery to reform a crushed foot. She packed immediately and left for Dublin.

If it were possible, Bernadette was more than ever pleased to see her. Her greeting was more like old times. More confidential. She had some rotten news. Beccy was not to be alarmed. George was still in hospital. He was on a 'drying-out course.' He had become dependent on alcohol and cocaine. They could visit him the next day.

It was difficult to locate him at first. He was not in any ward in the hospital but had been transferred to a house within the grounds. He was moving slowly about the garden on crutches when they first saw him. From a distance he looked as though he might be frail but otherwise recuperative.

The mother saw a shadow of her husband; the lover a man desperately needing help. Whether she could fulfill the role did not cross her mind.

They had tea together in the garden. He could, he said, discharge himself whenever he liked, but the authorities had cautioned against this. They had had him in before; he had left without completing the treatment and had been warned he would not be admitted again if he left without permission. The doctor had said after examining his toes and ankle that everything would probably heal satisfactorily within six or seven weeks and that it would not be wise to undergo surgery. He should stay at the centre for another week.

Beccy visited him each day and witnessed his all-round physical improvement. At the end of the week the two women brought him home. It was taking far longer for him to make a full recovery than they had expected. Beccy stayed until the middle of December. Her own folk were not clamouring but they dearly wanted to see her. In the event George decided she could not be allowed to travel alone to London and joined her.

He found the Hampstead Road premises cramped and the stairs difficult to negotiate. He had discarded crutches but still needed a stick to ease the pain off one foot. Beccy was rather saddened by his general attitude. She thought that with his education, training and recent experience of life he would have been prepared for any exigency, but he found her family strangely challenging and he was not equipped at the present to cope with much challenge. Beccy was inwardly embarrassed that he found them all so parochial, especially as she knew his chosen epithet to be quite wrongly applied. Of course they were financially poor by his standards and they were almost totally absorbed in the business.

"A rather messy, hand-to-mouth existence." he said.

In reality their trade had continued to prosper and the hand-to-mouth experience had not applied for some years. It was difficult for Leo and Rachel to change their old habits which were naturally frugal. But their lives seemed narrow and seedy to George, who was used to more space with rooms of his own; elegant if not exactly luxurious. He behaved like a fish out of water.

"This kitchen will be the death of me," he said with some seriousness. "I've got claustrophobia crushing my head." he confided to Beccy, and he reached out his wide arms blocking the narrow doorway.

True, everyone was more or less confined to the kitchen and semi-basement dining room. And in there Rachel had tried to disguise the iron-cage beds as decorative shelving, but they remained cumbersome and ugly and there was no option but to keep them. They had been gainfully employed on many occasions. George wanted to go out; to any theatres still showing, but taxis were almost non-existent and he could not manage walking to and from the buses. He wanted to get Beccy away again, quickly. Leo and Rachel understood and did not wish in any way to be the cause of tension between them.

After only four days Beccy agreed to go back to Ireland. She made a fleeting visit to Gadsden and they departed. Leo and Rachel stood together on the upper steps of the house and shyly waved them off.

Chapter Forty-Nine

It was not until April of 1945 that Beccy returned to London. Rachel and Leo had already known but it still came as a shock to them to have full realisation of Beccy's condition. She was five months pregnant. George had not accompanied her.

"He is not at all well, and certainly not up to the journey," she said.

Beccy, aware now as never before of her body, immersed herself into the all-protective shell at Hampstead Road. Leo was bewildered and uncomprehending. It was the war, he convinced himself. It ruined the lives of many who came through it. They, of course, would make the best of prevailing conditions. But, in reality, when it came to personal relationships he leaned heavily upon Rachel. And at the moment, she was more worried about Beccy's general health than the fact of her pregnancy; she was so thin and seemed to her to be undernourished. Owing to food shortages special effort was needed to make appetising meals but Rachel rose to the occasion and enjoyed having a special reason to concentrate on cooking. Beccy's obvious need of care did focus attention, but she was not demanding and enjoyed, as ever, the ambience of home.

Tom, home on short leave, had come to visit his favourite people. He had not known Beccy was to be present and he was quite visibly shocked when he saw her. He was a great favourite of Rachel's and she felt deeply for him. Beccy was open with Tom. She had known him for so long she could not have spoken to him indirectly.

"George is a sick man at the moment. He insisted I came home for a while. I shall be returning at the end of the week. He needs me, Tom."

It was obvious Tom thought she was beautiful and he loved her from the depth of his being. He did his best to help around the house but it was as though his leave pass burnt a hole in his pocket. He could not concentrate, and Beccy worried him. He longed to be a civilian again and was making plans to join the building industry. He had already located an established builder in Fortress Road who had agreed to accept him as a partner. Tom had pledged all his gratuity and savings to the project.

Joe came to stay for a few days and was glad to discuss his plans with Tom. Having qualified as an engineering draughtsman Joe was projecting his thoughts to the immediate post-war period and wondered if he should try to make the transfer to architecture.

"Would you consider working with me?" he asked Tom.

Tom outlined his own plans, but said he would give Joe's suggestion serious consideration. They both felt buoyed by their discussion. They had more than one iron in the fire and were ready to put their plans into practice when the final all-clear sounded.

Beccy went to see Dot at her new house, which she had not previously visited. Tom must have told her, yet her reaction on their meeting quite surprised Beccy. Dot seemed to be very embarrassed at first and regained her equanimity only after learning something of Beccy's partnership with Bernadette and her association with George. Beccy was very circumspect and completely omitted to speak of the French episode.

Beccy's week in London raced past.

"Much too short a stay," complained Rachel, not even registering that she had lapsed into German. She had already given Beccy a list of do's and don'ts. Most strictures concerned eating and resting.

"And always put your feet up when you sit. You can get plenty of milk in Dublin? Take care. Take care."

Leo accompanied her to the station. She kissed him. "Dear girl. We shall want to see the baby as soon as possible."

Beccy stood at the compartment window as the train pulled out. Leo waved in her direction but could not see her through his misted eyes.

Chapter Fifty

Bernadette met Beccy from the railway station and in the taxi she learned that George was not making satisfactory progress. He suffered from nightmares and deprived of sleep, had again turned to alcohol and drugs for solace. He tried to face up to his new responsibilities when he saw Beccy. He struggled to pull himself together but seemed to lack the resourcefulness he had shown in such abundance before the war. His foot had not improved as well as expected and he swung painfully on crutches to meet Beccy. It was obvious that he felt ashamed and inadequate. The strain showed on his face and demeanour, and he succumbed to bouts of severe despondency. The last few years had indelibly marked him. The subterfuges and double-dealings had reshaped his character, twisted his objectives and pulled his life irrevocably out of focus. He was, along with many others, a victim of wartime psychosis.

Three days after Beccy's return to Ireland she and Bernadette had to take George back to hospital. They were both alarmed. He seemed to be deteriorating by the hour. He was admitted immediately and put into a unit where he could receive special attention. The doctor said that owing to the patient's drug dependence the prognosis was complicated and he was not prepared to say how long he would be detained.

That night Bernadette was telephoned at home. An emergency had arisen. She and Beccy returned to the hospital. George had been moved into a single-bedded wing off the main ward. When Bernadette saw him she clasped Beccy's hand tightly and then left them together.

"Dear Beccy."

She had to put her head close to his to hear the whisper.

"I'm not going to pull through this one."

Despite the obvious gravity of the situation Beccy was unwilling to believe the evidence before her. The child moved inside her and she put George's hand on her stomach. He gave a smile of understanding and when Bernadette came in he had his head on Beccy's chest. Bernadette and a nurse had to help Beccy away. She made no sound or put up any resistance; it was just that she had become immobile, stiff-jointed and walking as though on stilts.

When at her home Bernadette wept openly. She shouldered an immense responsibility. Without a husband she had struggled to nurture and educate her lovely son. She blamed herself for his involvement in the Secret Service and to exacerbate her guilt now saw clearly other safer paths she could have guided him. She had Beccy to look after and found some solace in that. Beccy was too ill even to attend the funeral. She was drained of all emotion and could make no adequate response to Bernadette's solicitations. After a week she was medically sedated and subsequently removed to a gynaecological ward at the hospital.

She was falling, falling into a deep chasm. There was no light and no way to escape. The sides of the pit were close to her head but not touching as they raced past in her descent. She tried calling.

"Help me. Help me!" but no one lifted a finger. She called out: "Crouchon. Marcel Crouchon." Who was Crouchon? She had no idea. Her panic increased with her speed of falling. "Help, help!" She could barely get her throat around the word. Then in desperation she called "Jacques, I cannot do it." Still the blackness enveloped her. Then her stomach was being invaded, she was being torn apart. "George!" she screamed. And in a final agony of dark incomprehension a long wail, "G-e-o-r-g-e!"

She opened her eyes to the white. She was lying in the foetal position clutching her belly. Bernadette soothed her forehead with water of cologne. Beccy looked at her. Bernadette's face personified compassion; her tears at last relieving the turmoil. Beccy looked at her own body almost in disbelief.

She took Bernadette's willing hand and read the silence.

"Boy or girl?"

"Girl. You can see her later."

She remained in the ward for a week, after which Bernadette took her home. There was a letter from Rachel waiting for her in that Dublin house; a house permeated with deep trauma. Beccy had been advised, as though advice was necessary, to treat her condition with the utmost seriousness. She was tenderly nursed by Bernadette who felt Beccy was now her only life-line. She believed she would have suffered insanity had she not been so occupied.

Beccy was on her feet again in seven days, desperately struggling to make sense of her life. The more she grappled the more any possible relief from anxiety and guilt eluded her. At her worst moments she felt responsible for the loss of two lives, a man's and a little child's. She and Bernadette had individual yet not linking problems to resolve. Perhaps they were insoluble but as the days turned to weeks a partial healing ensued.

Neither women could define a point in time but they did realise that through their mutual suffering they were heavily dependent on each other. No one and nothing could administer to their emotional needs. They alone were the creators and the potential conduits of resolution. Through adversity their lives had become indissolubly combined.

It was not until nearly three weeks later that the women were able to weighthe improfitability of dwelling too much in the past. The war in Europe was ending and they had to reconstruct their careers to survive.

Chapter Fifty-One

Tom's was one of the first groups to receive the demobilisation orders. It did not come too soon for him, and upon release he made an immediate visit to his mother's house. He had thought it a match box when she first moved there. Now it felt too small to allow him to breathe. His first enquiries, as usual, concerned the Radstones.

When Dot gave him the latest information he hurried across to Hampstead Road. He found Leo and Rachel distraught.

"I shall write immediately and ask to see her," said Tom.

"But your business Tom. You must attend to that first." Leo knew Tom would not be dissuaded. Rachel had no need to intervene. She knew Tom's character. He would go to Dublin, find out about Beccy at first hand and bring back a full report.

Tom visited Leo and Rachel everyday during the following week. He rarely stayed long owing to his business preparations, but at the end of the week he was able to say that he was on his way to Ireland. He had received a reply from Beccy to say that if he could spare the time he would be made very welcome at The Laurels.

Tom stayed eight days in Dublin and returned to Leo and Rachel with a full report.

Chapter Fifty-Two

The European market in art no longer existed in any viable form. There were still treasured artefacts waiting to change hands but Bernadette had calculated it would be years before it would be possible to effect any business there. In any case, she guessed, the direction of trade might well turn out to be in the opposite way; from England through the Low Countries and on to Germany. She now wanted to return to London as soon as possible, because that was still the centre of the artworld. She was negotiating for property near to St. John's Wood. They had both found this to be a convenient centre in the earlier days.

By the late autumn of 1945 they had found a flat in Gloucester Terrace. There appeared to be no structural damage but the inside of the building had been left in very poor condition. Beccy applied for the necessary permits to allow restoration to the property, which were readily granted. Then she arranged for tenders. Beccy consulted Tom about the repairs to the property and as usual he was a pillar of support. Robert Moser too had been demobilised early. He had taken up the reins of his business quickly and he put himself at the women's disposal in his spare moments. They were grateful for his business acumen and the property repairs were accomplished under licence; austere but workman-like.

The bedroom windows of the flat overlooked the park and from her window Beccy could see to Sussex Place. After her long recuperation she was at last able to smile, and as she looked out it amused her to think she no longer had to be confronted with a mountain of potatoes. It was while glancing from this window that she saw Robert draw up. His car had been in dry-dock while he had been away on Active Service and now Beccy thought he seemed pleased to have its use again, limited though it was by petrol rationing. He had become a fairly frequent caller, often unannounced, since the renovation of Bernadette's flat.

Robert liked calling. He had seen Beccy develop from a gangling youth to a mature woman. Despite her experiences, she could not be called 'worldly' as Bernadette was, but their characters complimented each others and Robert had been intrigued to witness the growth of their business partnership.

Beccy knew Robert had opened two other business premises to help with the increase in orders for clothing. They were both situated near to Soho and each was considerably larger than the one run by her father. Robert had put a manageress into each of these premises and they were prospering. He left the heavier clothing in the capable hands of Leo and Rachel but he had the foresight to realise that London was tired of austerity. Clothing coupons or no, women wanted to look smarter, lighter, and even frivolous. Most people had no spare money so he did not try to compete with the houses of haute couture, but studied the cheaper markets as being developed in America. The United States had not suffered deprivation on a scale seen in Europe and they were encouraging a culture of shopping which seemed to be grossly extravagant when viewed from this side of the Atlantic. Beccy was not surprised to see how quickly Robert had spotted the potential, but she was amazed he had so quickly arranged to visit his cousin in Peterson, New Jersey.

"I was flabbergasted," he said. "The pace of life and the colour and the speed! But you've seen it all, Bernadette. I tried to remember dress shapes, hem lengths and styles. Look! I've done a few scribbles," and he produced some rather shaky sketches. This is what he had in mind in calling at Gloucester Terrace today. And he really enjoyed the women's company.

"Why don't you two explore the American market? It's bustling, and ready money is available for antiques." Bernadette sat up. She knew about antiques, and something of American ways. Robert was still talking: "I'm going back to New Jersey at the end of the month. Come with me and see for yourselves."

When he left, the women sat back and chuckled. And then they realised they had not felt light-hearted for a long time.

"He's a tonic. He's breezy and uncomplicated. I like him," said Bernadette; "He's modest too. During the war he was decorated with the Distinguished Service Order. I read about it in the London Gazette."

Robert had steadfastly refused to talk about it. He would not be drawn on the subject. For him the war was mercifully over, and he was not going to waver in the pursuance of his career.

"America?" they said to each other.

"Go west, young woman."

"Well you must come too."

And then they tried serious conversation. How could they manage introductions? Bernadette was not bereft in this department and she had about three weeks to make a suitable plan of campaign. She left all the bookkeeping to Beccy, who established they could afford the project, whether the initial outcome was profitable or not.

In the event, their journey to America was successful and enjoyable. They stayed in Paterson but had two days and nights in New York. They made several contacts and compiled quite a long list of items the dealers would be glad to accept. In addition Bernadette found her expertise had been greatly appreciated by one private buyer who sought a piece of 18th Century Wedgwood for his own collection.

They saw little of Robert but joined him for the return journey. He was not particularly communicative but did say that he thought he had the feel of the new trends and expected to return when he had tested his theory on the home market.

The women had to decide whether the America project would become profitable. It seemed incredulous that profit could be made on such a small turn-over. They wondered if they might be able to develop the business so that all but the most precious articles could be crated rather than hand-carried.

During the next few weeks they attended sales around the country. The London showrooms were taking longer to recover than those in the provinces. Gradually they collected the articles itemised on their New York list. They despatched several lots; the money was telegraphed to their bank and gradually a small but steady course of income was maintained. Meanwhile they searched for articles of special interest or rarity, much as they had done in Berlin years ago. They found this aspect of the business far more interesting and tried to concentrate on the more esoteric corner of the market.

Leo and Rachel were delighted whenever Beccy called in. Her visits had been less regular lately and the longer intervals had reinforced for them her steady progress in recovery. They were pleased to see her beginning to look her old radiant self.

Robert was often at Hampstead Road although he was called away, nowadays, more often to Soho. He had made some important decisions and wished to confer with Leo and Rachel. He wished to make over the whole business here to them. They were to do with it exactly as they thought fit.

"I want you to be quite independent of me. It's yours complete. I have engaged a solicitor to draw up the deeds."

They were taken aback. They were both beginning to feel their age and this suggestion had come as a complete surprise.

"I'll always be around if you want my help."

Leo knew that Robert was successful with his main enterprise and that there was less demand for heavy clothing. Perhaps they could carry on gently until retirement. Rachel smiled and thought Leo would never retire. Robert had not finished.

"The deeds of the house will, naturally, come with the business. It's all covered in the legal documents."

The offer was more than generous and it was now their turn to look for guidance. They turned to Beccy.

"May I consult Bernadette?" she asked.

When Robert had left that evening they were pleased to have their deliberations interrupted by a flying visit from Tom. Tom's affairs had not succeeded as he had hoped. In place of his usual optimism he looked sad. The projected partnership, on which he had placed such hope, had not transpired. They all felt very sorry for Tom, who was such a favourite at Hampstead Road. Beccy felt very sorry for him and accompanied him back to Chalk Farm. She would be glad to see Dot. They walked arm in arm in the darkness.

Suddenly Tom said, "You know I love you. And I've asked you before but would you consider marrying me?"

Beccy halted in her stride. She always was fond of Tom. They were like affectionate brother and sister. She could not however imagine, had certainly never considered living with him, even though he had broached the subject before. She felt vulnerable now because his affairs were so astray.

"Sorry I was so blunt," said Tom, who could not be blunt. "May I ask you another time?"

Beccy was glad of the breathing space. Then she dismissed this thought as cowardly.

"Please Tom! Don't ask me."

Beccy retraced her steps toward Gloucester Terrace. She no longer felt inclined to talk to Dot this night. Tom insisted on accompanying her. When they arrived at the flat she thanked Tom for everything. She did not invite him in, nor would she go in. He was forced to leave her at the gate and she watched as he walked sadly away through the park, a route he had taken on so many previous occasions.

Chapter Fifty-Three

Robert was preparing for another journey to the States. He asked the women whether they would come with him again. "Can either of you sketch? I can't get my staff to draw a model."

Bernadette immediately denied any ability in that direction.

"I used to see you wielding a soft pencil," she said to Beccy, "Try it!"

"Could you practise it in time for February? I'm going in the winter time when they will be showing their summer clothes. Come?"

It reminded Beccy of her one appearance on the cat-walk.

"Yes, that sweet black cat," said Bernadette.

"Come and sketch. Then we'll have a couple of day's holiday."

"Shall we?" Beccy looked at Bernadette.

"I'll have to think about it."

When Robert left, Bernadette took up the subject straight away.

"You go. I won't come this time."

Beccy stared at her.

"No need to look like that, madam. You know what I mean."

Beccy blushed to the roots of her hair, She had regrown her hair to just below collar-line and it looked lustrously beautiful. She forced an immediate diversion by telling about the proposed transfer of deeds at Hampstead Road.

"Yes, he's generous as well," said Bernadette. "I think Leo and

Rachel would be wise seriously to consider the offer. They have worked tremendously hard for the business. They should have their share of the profits."

Beccy resolved to see her parents very soon to gauge their reaction. Privately she thought they would not accept the offer as a gift, but might be persuaded, as Bernadette had suggested, that it was a natural development of the original contract.

She did go to America with Robert. Her sketching had improved and she was able to put the skill to some use. She saw another side to her escort. She knew him as a dynamic man but had not realised how very considerate he could be. He was kind and very anxious for her welfare. After the business of the day concluded, he deferred to her wishes and they enjoyed each other's company. As planned they had two day's holiday. One evening they dined on Broadway before going to the theatre and on the second day they explored downtown Manhattan. It was exciting and fresh, particularly after the constraints of post war Britain. Robert's cousin was a warm hearted host. He had treated them royally and far from censoring her efforts had encouraged Beccy to follow some of his designs. And he was able to nudge Robert in the direction of the fashion's possible trend.

On their return Bernadette wanted to know of progress. Beccy undid her folder of sketches.

"I don't mean the sketches! I know you are good at that."

Beccy fingered her work and considered how they might look made up.

"I mean," persisted Bernadette. "You know what I mean. You and Robert?"

Robert had certainly known the women for a long time. They enjoyed his company, where so much could be taken for granted. It made their relationship comfortable and easy. Bernadette had watched Robert's subtle courtship with growing interest. They were so well suited, she thought; intelligent, thoughtful and generous.

"You have had a good holiday!"

"It was splendid," said Beccy. "And yes," she added quickly, "Robert is a fine man. I had not *seen* him before. He always appeared to be so preoccupied with business. He's lovely off duty!"

"And?" enquired Bernadette.

It was not for another week that Beccy was able to oblige

Bernadette with the information she wanted.

"Yes. We intend to be married. Soon as possible. The briefest engagement."

Bernadette hugged her and held her for a long time.

"Is Rachel pleased?"

"We are going to tell them this evening."

Chapter Fifty-Four

Robert told Beccy he wanted to live in a house overlooking the park. Beccy had always enjoyed Regent's Park but said she would dearly love a change of venue. Then Robert said mischievously, "How about Hyde Park?"

They found a very small but suitable flat in Kensington Road. Robert had achieved his two most cherished ambitions: he had won Beccy, and he was well established in a profitable business.

He proved to be a most considerate husband. He loved his new status, and he and Beccy proved to be stable partners. She retained close contact with Bernadette, did not relinquish her post as keeper of the books and to Bernadette's great delight was able to accompany her on occasional forays. When they had been married for three months, and Bernadette could see how they thrived on each other's company, she called on them at Kensington Road. She had visited before and on each occasion had brought them a small gift: a little woodcut, a piece of Venetian glass, an old tapestry she had brought from Ireland. Today she had a small wooden box.

When alone with Beccy she said, "You know what is here. Please have them. He so wished them for you. When we went in search of them all those years ago he asked me to renegotiate with the prospective buyer so that he could present them to you."

Beccy experienced difficult, conflicting emotions. Her graciousness prevailed. She carefully untied the box and removed the vases. She smoothed the cold porcelain to her face and said, "They need warmth, you see."

Beccy could not recall days of such happiness. On looking back she had enjoyed the serenity and love of family. They had lived mostly in poverty but they had always been rich in understanding. But now she had a positive role to play in contributing to their joint welfare. Her marriage had become firmly established, she and Robert sought the same aims and their love had grown alongside real friendship. Robert was so vital in everything she did and had a genuine involvement in Beccy's affairs. He never interfered, but when asked, usually made observations that crucially affected her decisions.

However, he was not a handyman in the house. (He had to employ a plumber to renew a tap washer.) He erected no shelves for Beccy's books, some of which were now in a cabinet; most however, lined the floor. He certainly did not trust his very limited ability in carpentry to make a shelf for the precious vases. They graced the dressing table pending provision more in accordance with their elegance. Ironically it might have been their presence in the bedroom which brought on a bout of nightmares which dogged her for short but concentrated periods. Robert had learned of some of her trials and understood that full recuperation would probably take a long while, but he was alarmed at her dreaming convulsions. One recurring vision, she told him, was of being snatched from Jacques when she was frozen with terror on Hardelot Plage.

She could not get him out of her mind and she determined to enlist her husband's expertise in moving mountains. She must find Jacques if only to exorcise her ghosts. Robert required all the detailed circumstances. He had heard them several times but thought their repetition would help to relieve Beccy's fear. He had acquired some knowledge of Northern France as an active Sapper and could but feel pessimistic of Jacques' survival. He did not convey this impression to Beccy. At heart he was an optimist, and with experience in the mercurial world of business, always showed the positive side of a debate to clients and competitors alike.

Beccy was cheered when Robert was enlisted to her cause. He recognised that a courageous man working alone would perhaps have a better change of survival than the average soldier, and he tried to envisage Jacques' strategy. Beccy had maintained a regular correspondence with Danny who had removed to Whitehall from Gadsden but an informative letter recently came as something of a surprise. Danny could report nothing of Jacques' immediate whereabouts but he had been positively sighted near the little town of Montreuil. That was in December of 1945. She regretted she had no more recent information. Beccy was mildly encouraged by the news and thought the date of the sighting to be positively hopeful.

Bernadette was happy to agree that Beccy should have a holiday but was disappointed to know they intended to spend the time touring northern France.

Robert's old Morris Ten had been secured in a garage during his time in the Services and had subsequently been overhauled. In February of 1947 Beccy and he crossed the Channel to Calais on a converted frigate. The car was hoisted aboard by crane and driven over makeshift ramps by a crew member. They took the coast road to Boulogne and Le Touquet. They stopped the car near to Neufchatel and looked across to Hameau and the sea. Beccy held Robert's arm tightly and in a strangely cold monotone retold, in a few words, the events of the terrible night when she had last seen Jacques. Robert hurried her back to the car and wrapped a blanket round her.

They moved on to Étaples and stayed at a hotel in Montreuil. They had only a name to go on. It was probably the right one because he had always said: "Just call me Jacques", suggesting a life-long familiarity. But Beccy felt sure of nothing.

When they spoke of "Le Maquis" at the hotel or tried to broach the subject of the Resistance their enquiries were largely met with a blank stare or a disinclination to be drawn. One person however, remembered that before the invasion, Lysanders had landed near to a little place called Fressin. Robert and Beccy hastened off to explore that village and at the café the proprietor laughed when they mentioned the name Jacques. But he clearly remembered several members of the Maquis being rounded up before the war ended. They were certainly taken to the East, probably to Germany; he knew no more.

Fighting against every rational instinct Beccy implored Robert to drive to Lille. They took two days to get there, having stopped overnight at Bethune. They drove around the streets of Lille gradually getting closer to the city centre. A tremendous amount of havoc had been wrought. Many buildings had been completely destroyed and they saw whole streets being cleared in preparation for new building.

They pulled in close to the Town Hall. It was covered in wooden scaffolding, but judging by the hessian awning, business was being transacted. They entered and approached the information desk. A pretty young woman asked their business. They had to raise their voices above the banging and shouting of the decorators who seemed to be everywhere on ladders and on temporary plank- galleries. Beccy asked if she could be directed to anyone with experience of the local Maquis. The clerk was totally uncomprehending. Beccy felt inadequate and suddenly ridiculous. They turned to go, and clutching at straws Robert asked an elderly man who was sweeping with a large broom in an effort to keep the floor clear of the workmen's debris, the same question. He either did not know or was afraid to answer. He gave a Gallic shrug.

"It was wartime, monsieur," he said as though logically concluding an argument.

Deflated and cold they returned to the car. Robert bought petrol and wondered, not for the first time, how it came to be in plentiful supply when it was stringently rationed at home. As they drove back toward Calais Beccy showed Robert the little turning on the right to St. Bernard. From the car the roads looked different but they parked in the little street and on foot looked for the café. Nothing much seemed to have changed and yet it did not look familiar to her. She crossed the road and stared directly at the only café. No, she could not honestly say she recognised it. They recrossed and entered and as the door bell clanged it sent a shock through her body.

An elderly woman stood behind the bar and wished them Good day, and asked them if they would like something. Robert asked for two glasses of lemonade. They took their drinks and sat at a marble-topped table. Beside them was an elderly man smoking a Gauloise. He puffed in their direction and Beccy asked him if the proprietor was about.

"There's the proprietress," he said. "Lost her husband in Germany." He pointed a finger to his head. "Toc, toc, you know, a bit simple."

She and Robert rose to leave, and as they got to the counter Beccy reached her hand across. Why hadn't they recognised each other? The old woman clasped Beccy's hand and smiled.

"I was here during the war," she said looking straight into the woman's eyes.

"Oh, the war," said the woman.

Beccy rolled up her sleeve and revealed a long scar on her forearm. The woman's fingers touched it gently.

"Remember?" said Beccy.

"Were you here when they took him away?"

Beccy could not remove her gaze. Then struggling to form the words over a constricted throat she whispered hoarsely: "No, I was not here that day."

"You were not here that day," echoed the Aunt.

"No." And still struggling for control Beccy said "Do you know what became of Jacques?"

"Oh yes. He was here. They were all here then."

Beccy lowered her eyes. Robert left the café and the door bell clanged. The older woman stifled a sob as her head sank to her chest. They released their hands and the older woman said very softly; "They tell me I have not been well."

A customer came to be served and as the woman left Beccy to go to him she turned her head and said cheerfully: "Please come again."

Beccy sat in the car and wept. She owed such a great deal to the people here which she could never repay. She had learned no news of Jacques. Robert put his arm around her.

They drove back to Calais. They had embarked on a ludicrous search. They felt beaten and Robert was particularly humbled. He was not used to defeat, and this new experience was to haunt him. And now he could not imagine how he could ever have elevated his simple plan to a 'strategy.'

The short sea crossing was wearying and they headed for Canterbury and stayed overnight in a hotel. At dinner that evening they were attended by a charming young Frenchman who said his name was Jacques. He had no idea why the revelation of his name caused a mild intake of breath at the table.

Bernadette was the first to visit them after their tour of northern France. It was barely a fortnight since they had been together and Bernadette noticed how fatigued Beccy seemed to be. She put it down

180

to travel weariness and listened carefully to their pathetic goose-chase. She had clearly imagined it would be unprofitable but had said nothing to discourage them. She hoped that they had now put the quest behind them and that the matter had been laid to rest. She, herself, was bubbling with plans, and could hardly wait for them to finish their discourse. She had fully intended to give Beccy all the details but now she had second thoughts. In their prevailing mood she thought it inappropriate to mention the matter for the time being.

Robert was very glad to immerse himself in his business affairs. He was pleased to see it had been handled well in his absence. His ideas for meeting the new demand for livelier, breezier clothing for the younger generation had fallen on fertile soil. He had even managed to persuade Leo that men too were becoming more clothes-conscious. The epoch of 'make do and mend' was being buried with war detritus, and with the rejuvenation of industry began a new regard for money and what it could buy.

Chapter Fifty-Five

In the spring of 1948 Beccy was confined to hospital. Her baby was not due for three weeks but she had been advised to take special precaution. Everything went well. A boy was born in the early hours of the morning.

Robert had taken advantage of the liberalisation of hospital rules and had been with Beccy during the labour. All three of them were resting when Rachel and Leo came in to rejoice with them at noon that day. They were overjoyed to have a grandson. Beccy felt a small twinge of guilt when eventually the nurse suggested Beccy had probably had a long enough visit and encouraged Leo and Rachel to leave.

"Come back tomorrow. The boy will see you tomorrow."

They made lingering farewells as though tomorrow was too far away to contemplate and made their way home.

They had not been in long when they opened the door to a stranger's knocking. He was a heavily built man of about thirty-five years. He apologised for his accent and the intrusion but he had arrived here after much searching and was looking for Miss Rebecca Radstone. She was not available, Leo cheerfully explained, she had delivered a beautiful baby boy only a few hours ago. Who was he?

The man smiled and gave a tiny packet to Leo and asked if it might be presented to the lady when she was feeling strong enough to accept it. Rachel invited him in; he had a cup of tea but stayed only long enough to tell that he had wartime association with their daughter. Leo and Rachel were pleased to have his company but did not quite know how to respond as he would not expand upon the association. But with their natural courtesy they asked how long he was staying in the country and that perhaps he would be able to see Beccy in a few days' time. He explained that he had to leave for home that evening and with rather a sad smile he bade them farewell.

The following day Leo applied himself to his work with even greater diligence than ever. He did not want the time to lag and it was as much as Rachel could do to keep the man at the table long enough to have a meal. But she too was glad to be among the first at the hospital for visiting time. The boy did see them; with wide blue eyes that looked rather sternly as though they had kept him waiting unnecessarily. But having seen them he turned his head to his mother and closed his eyes.

They were allowed to stay for one hour whose dimension stretched and shrank according to the individual's viewpoint. Robert was so tired he hardly raised his head from his chest and the sound of quiet chatter made an appropriate background for his dreams. Beccy and the boy lay back peacefully. Never a classic beauty, she now looked quite radiant. Rachel had brought some flowers and had been directed to a store-room to find a vase. Leo had brought the little packet in his coat pocket and was undecided about presenting it. It was nearly time for them to leave when Rachel returned. She looked so lovely to Leo as she bent to kiss the baby.

"This was delivered by hand yesterday," and Leo went on to explain with what details he had.

Beccy opened the packet and found the tiniest bottle of perfume. The little note attached said simply 'With love from Jacques.'

Chapter Fifty-Six

Bernadette had made quite elaborate plans to develop her contacts in America. She had again visited New York and was familiarising herself with the methods of business in the States. She was convinced there was enough potential profit to keep Beccy in partnership if her family commitments allowed. Beccy willingly agreed provided she could confine herself to the bookwork. Having a baby in the family had turned everything upside down. But she thought she could manage the accounts. Robert was not at all sure, although he had to admit that she had assumed the role of nurturing parent with apparent ease. Beccy sometimes imagined Robert to be guilty of a little over-protectiveness. All in all though, they judged themselves to be coping reasonably well.

Leo and Rachel lived only two short bus rides from Hampstead Road and Rachel availed herself of every opportunity to be with the baby. He was called John. He loved his grandparents, who in turn doted on him, and even Leo found his work sufficiently less demanding for him to be able to spend one day a week in his company. With the additional attention of loving Uncle Joe the boy thrived and developed strongly. He became as familiar with the Hampstead Road house as his own and loved to be trotted around the workshop rooms. The grandparents had a strong, encouraging influence on Little John and he was quite happy to be left with them for a day.

When Bernadette returned from New York she wondered whether Beccy could assist her on a two-day engagement in Edinburgh. They were to take the overnight train, search for some special pieces of pewter, stay the night in a hotel and return by the evening of the following day. And it transpired to be a great success. The dealer had been business-like and the appropriate set of tankards had been collected intact.

The travelling had been without incident and when Beccy hurried back to Hampstead Road she found a happy and tranquil little boy awaiting. He clung to her neck for a while but soon rejoined his Grandpa in the workroom.

It was as though Rachel and Beccy had not met for some months rather than two days. Rachel was able to answer most of Beccy's questions and accounted in some detail the boy's every move and utterance. Then they enjoyed a magnificent, confidential giggle when they came to earth realising the dimensions of this new life.

The family bond was strong and was reinforced that evening when Robert and Joseph arrived. Joe was beginning a short holiday. He had not managed to transfer from draughtsmanship and was not yet persuaded that Tom Fisher would make a successful partner in the building industry. He was, as everyone knew, an honest and reliable man, but whether he could amalgamate his talents to accommodate a larger organisation remained a doubt in Joe's mind. Joe even wondered whether he was the right man to organise a successful business. They sought advice from Robert, who had that indefinable but unmistakable quality of leadership. Generous as ever he gave them his ear and his time. More practical help he could not offer at the moment, as his own business was now extended as far as it could go within the present resources. But he seemed to be indefatigable, and they accepted his invitation to keep him informed of their respective plans. They were all willing and able to discuss their problems openly. This led to general harmony, was an antidote to formality and communication of ideas was speedy.

Whenever the whole tribe assembled at Hampstead Road the spectrum of family life, with its joys and frustrations, was enacted. Little John, brought up in this atmosphere of camaraderie and discussion became very forward in speech and learned early on that usually one person spoke at a time while the other listened. At the age of three he was a most socialised little boy who gave the impression of looking around solicitously to see if everyone was present at the supper table. So "Where is Uncle Joe, Uncle Tom, Auntie Dot, or Auntie Bernie?", became a customary phrase.

Beccy found she was able to accompany Bernadette quite often nowadays, but rarely extended her absence beyond one night. On one occasion she had to travel only as far as Swindon, where the women were listing steam-railway memorabilia. They took John with them, successfully completed their assignment, stayed in a hotel and were back in London by noon the next day. It was not an experience that could often have been repeated. John enjoyed the train journey rather more than his mother who had a very grubby dishevelled boy to clean up on arrival.

On another occasion Beccy went to Stoke to order a special set of modern Wedgwood for an American client. She had persuaded Robert to take them in the new car. She sat on the back seat with the boy and they all enjoyed the visit and the overnight stop at Ironbridge. It was all so easy and successful that the parents thought they could manage a travelling holiday. Like most other subjects, this notion was mentioned at Rachel's supper table.

Chapter Fifty-Seven

The flat in Kensington Road was now comfortable and familiar. It was furnished without ostentation and with few ornaments or pictures. The Dresden vases now had pride of place in the sitting room and from their corner niche added an air of elegance to the general atmosphere and were greatly admired. Robert had come to see them as beautiful objects, and for Beccy, quite naturally, there were stronger connotations. When their presence caught her unaware she was arrested and had to give them time. They were substantive proof of critical markers which had affected her life. She often wondered if she could ever repay, even in a small way, the debt she owed to so many people. And she reluctantly concluded that it was an impossible dream. The only thing she could do would be symbolic. But could she make even that gesture?

Her thoughts turned to Germany and to Frau Hugel. Had she survived the war? She remembered her dignity and courage when she had spoken of her hopes and longings for her family's emigration to America. Beccy felt such gratitude for the joy of her husband, her child and extended family she became overwhelmed as of a surfeit of blessings.

Beccy wondered if it would be possible to arrange a holiday in Berlin. Robert concurred immediately and Rachel rather surprisingly expressed her willingness to join them if they thought it would be helpful or of course she would have Johnny if they preferred to go by themselves. Leo could not be persuaded to have a holiday and least of all to Germany, wild horses couldn't drag him there. But their plans were eventually resolved. Rachel would join them and would be fulfilled looking after her grandson; they would sit together on the back seat of the car, play games and thoroughly enjoy each other's company. They planned to have four full days in Berlin and if the opportunity presented itself Rachel would make a search for her mother's gravestone.

It would most assuredly be her last opportunity.

Robert and Beccy were to share the driving. She was the experienced negotiator and instigator of the project. Her aim was clear. Robert was satisfied to have a few days away from business matters, and while fully supporting Beccy's quest had serious reservations about it receiving a satisfactory conclusion. Their abortive search in France for Jacques had been a salutary lesson to him and humbled him on recollection. He would concentrate on the navigation and general welfare of the passengers.

No lodgings had been pre-booked so that the excursion, to some extent, allowed flexibility. They expected to manage no more than a hundred and fifty miles each day on the outward journey. In the event this target was achieved, and they arrived in Berlin without mishap and not too travel-weary. Little John was getting quite used to staying in hotels and at the age of four happily slept with his grandmother or with his parents. It proved to be a most congenial arrangement. Beccy did not attempt to put the boy to bed early. He remained up for the evening meal, after which they managed a short walk in the park.

It was on the first evening's walk across Victoria Park that Beccy resolved to begin her search for Frau Hugel in the morning. Rachel said she would try to find her mother's last resting place. The women were to explore independently while Robert looked after the boy. The plan was unanimously agreed; they would meet in the evening.

In the morning Beccy walked across the park. Despite obvious signs of lingering war-time damage, rapid progress was being made toward the reconstruction of Berlin. Remarkably, the block of flats where she had met Frau Hugel all those years ago was still intact. It looked very shabby and badly scarred. She could not find a janitor but made her way unerringly to the apartment where she had first seen the Dresden vases. At the door her resolve nearly failed. She took a deep breath and knocked. It was answered by a cautious opening. So far as Beccy could see her the figure presented a stooped elderly woman. At first her imagination leaped the barriers and she spoke as if to address Frau Hugel. Frau Hugel was unknown however to the present occupant. No, she could not really help. No, there was no janitor these days; had not been since the war. At the mention of war, Beccy asked whether any of the residents had lived in the apartments before. The door had gradually opened little by little during this exchange, and deciding she was not about to be molested she invited the young woman inside.

Beccy recognised the room. She thought it had not even been decorated. It was brown and grimy. Then she wondered fleetingly at its miraculous survival. The old woman was willing to talk. She had lived here throughout the whole of the hostilities and she gave a graphic account of her experiences. She still had no notion at all regarding the Hugels. She had purchased the flat from local agents. Beccy made a note of the agent's address and as she stood to leave was informed of a man living in the basement who had been here for ages and was known to be a mine of local knowledge.

Beccy took her leave, descended the stone stairway past the ground floor and entered a dark corridor which she hoped would lead to the basement apartments. She had to negotiate another flight. Through the gloom she could just manage to make out a door knocker. A man answered the knock and squinted at her. The person she was probably seeking lived two doors away; he had no idea whether he was at home. She found the door to which the man had pointed and banged on it with her fist. It was eventually opened by a man leaning on a stick. He asked what she wanted.

Yes, he had known the Hugel family. Herr Hugel had been a friend. Died in 1933. Left a widow and a son. The son went to America, to Pennsylvania he had heard. Old lady Hugel went back to the family home in Dresden to live with her sister. They had both been killed in the raid. The man spoke in asthmatic staccato and was brief.

Beccy was very saddened by the information but was glad of his brevity because an awful stench emanated from the room. She retraced her steps, gasping for air, and walked rapidly through the park. She found the housing agency, and with meticulous efficiency they searched their files and were able to confirm they had, indeed, negotiated a sale for Frau Hugel. Beccy was elated with the discovery and felt she had firmly located a piece of her jig-saw puzzle. She hastened away to the Records Office. She wanted to double check the Hugel family's emigration and to see if there was a forwarding address.

The search took far longer than she had thought imaginable. To begin with, the clerk said she should give a few day's notice, but under the circumstances he would give her especial consideration. She waited; he presumably searched. A full hour later the filing clerk reappeared. He was almost as pleased as Beccy when he reported he had found the entry for Herr and Frau Hugel and family, with the emigration date and the address for forward posting. Beccy jumped for joy, grasped the clerk's hand and thanked him so profusely he was quite embarrassed.

When they all met that day for the evening meal they compared notes. Rachel had been to the Friedhof Records and had received the name of only one cemetery where she might profitably look. She was not really disappointed because she had not placed much faith in success at the outset.

Robert and the boy had enjoyed their day. He did not often have his father's undivided attention, had made the most of the opportunity and had exhausted Robert with questions.

And Beccy's news pleased them all. She felt so lifted by her discoveries that her small victory was infectious and they revelled in her joy. She would stay with Robert and John tomorrow while Rachel continued her quest, which would take her to a Friedhof at Birkenwerder to the north of the city.

The following morning Robert took Rachel out to Birkenwerder. He offered to stay with her but she insisted on being alone.

"If I have found no positive lead by midday I shall return to the hotel. May see you there for lunch?"

"Doubt if we will be back before evening," said Robert. "Beccy has plans."

In fact she had no special plans. She was just very pleased to have her family quite to herself. They visited the zoological gardens and did some window shopping. Robert noted the clothing was largely American style; the type he wished to promote. He was very impressed with the displays and thought London had quite a lot to learn from this city which was quickly rising from the ashes. John was as intrigued as a four-year-old could be, and was very excited when they purchased an electric train which was operated by its own small battery.

By late afternoon they had all had quite enough and returned to the hotel. Rachel was there to greet them. She had drawn a blank and had decided to give up the search. She appeared tired; she had done her best and felt relieved of the need to make any more excursions.

As they went into the dining room the hotel porter brought a telegram addressed to Mrs. R. Moser. It read: "Confirmed address. Jacques Mouton-Liger. 14 Rue Jeanne d'Arc. St. Mande. Paris. Danny. STOP."

"Please let's go home through Paris."

"It must be five hundred miles."

"Can we manage it, Robert?"

"Well, we should have to stay a night in Frankfurt. Then make an early start to get to Paris the day after."

"Can it be done?"

"Then we should have to stay over in Paris. Might even have to stay two nights. What do you think, Rachel?"

Rachel had no opinion. She would be quite happy in the back with John. The only thing she queried was the extra time being spent away.

That night Robert sent a telegram to Leo: "Give us four more days. All well. Seeking Jacques. Love R, STOP."

They made an early morning start and beat the Berlin traffic jam. They drove steadily again sharing the driving and had a break at Leipzig and had their lunch at Weimar. They pulled in very late that evening at Frankfurt. And all went as planned the following day. They crossed Saarbrucken, stopped briefly at Metz and again at Chalons. Then as evening approached they entered Paris. It had been a great deal of travelling in two days and they were all glad when they were able to book in at the Miramar Hotel in the Boulevard Soult.

At breakfast Rachel declared herself to be quite refreshed and would take herself off by taxi to the Champs Elysées. Robert was very travel-weary and they agreed it would be best to stay here for another night. He and the child might walk to the lake later that day if the weather held.

Beccy appreciated her family's discretion and later that morning walked down the Rue de la Republique on her way to finding Jacques. She started off by walking quickly but as she neared her destination she slowed down appreciably. Before her was Jeanne d'Arc and she scanned the facades for house numbers. She came to a pair of large iron gates set in stone pillars. The gates were open and led into a courtyard surrounded on three sides by tall terraced houses. Number 14 was in the middle of the left-hand wing. Her feet felt leaden as they rang on the cobbled yard approaching the house. She was flustered now and the door knocker felt cold under her hand. She let it fall and it gently tapped its anvil. Presently she heard, above the thumping of her heart, heavy footsteps approaching the other side of the door. It opened wide.

"Hullo?", he said interrogatively.

He was a large man just as she had remembered. Darkly handsome and now bearded.

"Good morning," he said. Then he looked closer. "Madeleine." He pronounced each syllable slowly.

She held her hand out and he took it. Then he gently drew her toward him and kissed her on both cheeks.

"Madeleine," he said again. This time he extenuated the syllables even more. He drew her into the house. She had not spoken a word but continued to look at him. Then she hugged him with all her strength.

"Come," he said, gently releasing her.

She followed him up two long flights of stairs and into a room. She caught a strong whiff of turpentine, and saw standing at an easel, palette in hand, a woman of about her own age contemplating a painting.

"Good," said the woman. "You're just in time. I've got something to show you."

"And I've got something to show you," said Jacques.

The woman looked up.

"Yvette," said Jacques. "This is Madeleine."

That afternoon Robert and Beccy and John walked to Jeanne d'Arc. Yvette was downstairs standing in a large kitchen. She smiled in welcome and took John to peep into a cot standing by the window. He leaned over, lifted the baby's hand and examined her exquisite fingers.

"This is Beatrix," said Yvette, and the baby gurgled with the whole of her body.

That evening they all met again at the Miramar. Beccy said very little. She had rehearsed this meeting in her mind for years. Now, confronted with reality, she found the words to be inadequate. She had often shuddered to contemplate her fate had Jacques not rescued her from St. Bernard.

As they sat at dinner John rocked the pram. He was more interested in its occupant than in the proffered food. Robert was not at ease but Rachel, in halting French, managed to transcend any embarrassment. She had bought a box of cigars for Jacques that morning and now presented it to him.

"Thank you," said Jacques.

"No!" said Rachel firmly. "Thank you. Please come to see us again. You know where we live. You can leave Beatrix with me while you and Yvette explore."

Chapter Fifty-Eight

Leo had been extra busy while they were away. Unbeknown to Rachel he had arranged with Tom to bring his men to redecorate the kitchen and the dining room and to paint the front of the house. The first assignment had been achieved satisfactorily but Tom had underestimated the time factor, thus he was seen up an outside ladder when the family arrived. He called out. They all looked up and waved. Rachel was astonished to see the bright new kitchen with an aga standing proud and warm where once the old black-leaded stove had been. Leo grinned and said something about now they had the money.

Robert must have been privy to the secret because he stayed outside talking to Tom. Between climbing ladders and washing down paintwork he had managed to prepare the hot-pot which was simmering.

"To try the new stove," he said.

The homeward journey had exhausted the adults, but John was fully recovered and at supper that evening gave a glowing account of his holiday. He had enjoyed all the adventures, especially seeing Beatrix.

Robert and Beccy thought nothing could be as serene as Kensington Gardens that beautiful Sunday morning. Never had home felt so tranquil. John ran ahead to feed the ducks on the Round Pond. Happiness, that ephemeral state, could want no further expression.

They had undergone experiences, in a comparatively short span of time, denied to most of those from an earlier generation. Their knowledge of each other had deepened and they understood, as well as anyone is capable, the thoughts and aspirations of their partner. And their complementary characteristics formed the basis for the good relationship which parenthood had enhanced.

Beccy was now once again in the early stages of pregnancy, and they hoped it would be a girl. She felt extremely well and wished to continue working with Bernadette throughout the summer. On a few occasions, when they were not too busy, Beccy had taken John with her to Bernadette's flat in Gloucester Terrace and they had enjoyed a picnic in Regent's Park at midday. Bernadette had continued her communication with the American market and was planning another journey to New York. John heard all the planning arrangements as he watched his mother at the accounts books.

"How long will you be away?" he wanted to know. "Granny will be pleased to have me."

Bernadette understood this would very possibly be Beccy's last journey, for some years at least. She had extended her contacts to include a buyer in Newark. Beccy had an appointment in Harrisburg, Pennsylvania, some hundred and fifty miles from Newark. They decided to hire a car in America and reckoned that in six days they would be able to fulfill all their engagements.

Their plans were well laid, as usual, and the day before their departure Beccy had taken John to Hampstead Road. She hurried back to Kensington, to spend the evening with Robert.

Beccy had assiduously continued her search for the emigrant Hugels. She had written to the authorities in the U.S.A. and had received a reply giving their last known address. She had followed this lead quickly. Her letter had been forwarded to another address in Harrisburg and Herr Hugel had replied. Yes, he could remember Beccy quite well from that fateful day in Berlin. He remembered with gratitude her sympathetically listening to his mother's story. He thanked her for her condolence and would be very pleased to see her on her visit. He gave directions for finding them and said he would be at home with his wife to welcome her.

Beccy had regaled Bernadette with all her findings following her detailed account of their holiday in Germany and France. As ever,

Bernadette admired Beccy's thoroughness. She had eventually to accept her reasoning and agreed to include Harrisburg in their itinerary on the understanding that Beccy would undertake that leg of the assignment on her own.

Their flight to America proceeded without difficulty and they found the hired-car formalities ready for endorsement. They drove away from Kennedy and parked the car at their hotel in Newark, where they had booked for two nights.

Early next morning Beccy was anxious to depart for Harrisburg. She had put her small travelling bag on the back seat of the car next to the old hat box which Robert had helped her pack so carefully and which had to be unpacked for customs' inspection at New York. Now it was secure again and Bernadette could not resist a wistful glance. She did not say anything but gave Beccy a clinging hug and watched her as she drove away.

Beccy had learned the journey from the map and as soon as she had found her way out of Newark settled back for what she presumed would be a five hour drive. She made only one short stop en route for petrol and refreshment and arrived at Harrisburg in the early afternoon. There were some difficulties finding the address but after several enquiries was surprised to find herself outside a tenement block not unlike the quarters the Hugels had inhabited in Berlin. Once off the road, though, the dissimilarities became obvious. It was more to do with ambient noise and liveliness than with physical attributes. The children playing around wanted to carry her case and to show her the Hugels' flat. She held firmly to her hat box but was glad of the directions. A child knocked loudly at the door and called out; "Mr and Mrs Hugel, visitor!"

When the door closed on the apartment and the children were shut outside, Beccy suddenly felt overwhelmed. She had travelled thousands of miles and some long years preparing for this meeting. She sat on a chair and put a handkerchief to her face. Frau Hugel put a hand on her shoulder while her husband went away to make coffee. Freda Hugel and Beccy had not met before yet there was an instant affinity. Freda was the older and saw before her a pregnant young woman who had taken such pains to find them. David Hugel went downstairs to pay a couple of adolescents to keep their eyes on the motor car. They demanded twice what he offered, but said they would clean the car as well as look after it. He gave them a friendly slap and warned them of the dire consequences of letting him down.

The coffee revived Beccy, and with American hospitality, formalities were dispensed with and they took up their stories as though there had been a life-long friendship. After he had been in the U.S.A. for only one year David Hugel had pleaded with his mother to join them. They were struggling times and their accommodation was even poorer than the present arrangement. They had desperately wanted their mother to leave Germany. She had insisted she would be all right in Dresden, and as Beccy knew had gone to live with her sister. They were grave times for everyone, and the story proceeded to its inevitable conclusion. Beccy did not presume to burden them further by retelling her war-time history and was relieved they had not enquired about her business partner. The Hugels had two children, "All American," who were both at school. David said they regarded Europe as that far-off country of travail where their Grandmother had died.

As Beccy looked around she could see no sign of post-war prosperity and could but admire the fortitude of immigrants who had struggled against the odds to make a successful life for their families. She recognised the affinity between her own background and that of the Hugels and pictured, at that moment, her parents with her own son. Suddenly she turned to Robert for support. She had not anticipated these profound feelings and now felt lost without him. She rose from the chair and opened the old hat box.

"Please look in here," she asked as she removed the wrappings.

There they lay. Pristinely beautiful. In the quiet of the moment their eyes focused as one. As they stood by the little round table their hands touched lightly. There was silence, the silence of a sleepy afternoon. Then the sound of children playing outside brought them back to the present.

"Your mother would have wanted you to have them," she said simply. "Dresden china needs warmth."

No one touched the vases and they were still in the box when Beccy turned to leave.

She drove back to Newark that evening and did not disturb Bernadette when she got into bed shortly after midnight. She did not rise early; had not realised how tired she had become. Bernadette had the day's business arranged well in advance so that Beccy should not be too wearied. But Beccy was glad to be responsible for the afternoon's engagements. When their affairs were completed they returned to New York that evening and made preparations for the homeward journey.

The taxi had been directed to Gloucester Terrace via Kensington, and when it pulled in bedside Beccy's gate Bernadette did not alight. She waved through the taxi window to Robert and John who were already standing at the top of the outer steps. The taxi moved away into the stream of traffic. Beccy looked up at Robert. John had already raced down to her. Never had homecoming been so wonderful.